This book belongs to

POOLBEG

Other Books by Carolyn Swift

In this Series:

Robbers in the House
Robbers in the Hills
Robbers in the Town
Robbers in the Theatre
Robbers on the Streets
Robbers in a Merc

In Other Series:

Bugsy Goes to Limerick
Bugsy Goes to Cork
Bugsy Goes to Galway
Irish Myths and Tales
European Myths and Tales
The Secret City

For Adults:

Stage by Stage, Theatre Memoirs

ROBBERS ON T. V.

First published in 1989 by
Poolbeg Press Ltd
Knocksedan House,
Swords, Co Dublin, Ireland

Reprinted 1992

A catalogue record for this book is available from the British Library.

ISBN 1 85371 227 2

Cover design by Aileen Caffrey
Set by Print-Forme
Printed by Cox & Wyman Limited,
Reading, Berks.

ROBBERS
ON T. V.

Carolyn Swift

POOLBEG

For Bill Skinner

Who wrote the music for
"The Shadow Factory,"
in which this tale had its origins.

Camera Script

Fade up on Maura and widen to include
the group,
Mix to the Square, as Michael is put
through the hoop.

Two-shot of Maura and Whacker picking
up the track,
When you track in on Walkie-Talkie watch
your back.

Next, try a long shot, then zoom across to
pick up May,
Cut, thrust and super closing captions over
fray.

Contents

1

Fade Up on Maura

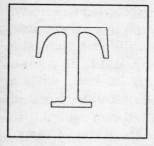he reception area already seemed full to bursting point with people as May Byrne pushed through the revolving doors of the Television Centre. She felt as nervous as if it were *she* who had to stand up in front of them all and sing.

"We'll never get through all these people," she said to her brother Richie. She would already have lost him in the crowd if his carroty-red hair did not serve as a beacon. "Let's go round to the stage door and wish Maura luck."

"There's no stage door," Richie replied and his pal Whacker added scornfully: "Do you never watch the *Late Late*? Even Gaybo goes in by this door. You're not in the Olympia now, you know."

"Then how are we gonna get through?" she

asked, but at that moment someone moved aside the barrier and the crowd started to surge forward. Showing their invitation cards to the security man, they passed through the doors in the inner wall and followed the crowd across a passage and through more doors into Studio 1. It looked quite different from the way it did on telly, May thought, as a man wearing ear-phones, which he used with a microphone as a sort of walkie-talkie, directed them up the steps of the wooden rostrum to places in the middle of the third row of seats.

She could see no-one else their age, but she soon forgot about that in the excitement of watching the men push cameras around. Then, as one swung directly towards them, Whacker gripped her arm.

"Look up there," he grinned, pointing, and May saw a television screen suspended above them, from which a second Whacker grinned back down at her. Beside him, she caught a glimpse of her own startled face before they both seemed to slide away, to be replaced by other faces, all grinning and waving.

"D'you think Imelda and Mickser spotted us? she whispered, for Maura had only been able to get three tickets and Whacker's sister and Mickser Dolan had had to settle for watching back home in the Square.

Whacker shook his head.

"They're only rehearsal pictures," he said. "Don't you know you never see the people without Gaybo being there?"

And suddenly there he was, looking smaller than she had expected, in his dark well-fitting suit that she guessed must have cost more than her father's and Mr Kelly's and Mr Dolan's and Mr Reilly's all put together. They all started to clap, but the familiar voice interrupted:

"You're very kind, very kind. But you're only going to have to do all that again in a minute, you know," and he began teasing a lady for sneaking a glance at her image on the television screen and pretending to have an argument with a man in the front row. Then, while they were all laughing at something he said about the Taoiseach that May did not really understand, she heard the drum roll they always played when they showed the picture of the owl at the start of the show, the man wearing the ear-phones waved at them to clap, a little red light glowed on top of the camera in front of May and again for a second she caught a glimpse of Richie and Whacker and herself in among all the others and knew that this time Imelda and Mickser would have seen them too, if they had happened to be looking in the right place at just that second.

"Enough! Enough!" Gaybo was crying, holding up his hand to stop the applause. "Tonight," he went on, "we have all sorts of interesting people here to introduce to you and, later on, we'll be having our usual little quiz just to make sure you're all awake, but first of all we're going to have a little music. Now, some of you may have seen the show in the Olympia last year about the Cattle-Raid of Cooley and the war between the men of Connacht and the men of Ulster and all that class of thing that we were taught at school, and you may remember a young Dublin girl who was making her very first stage appearance as the servant of Queen Maeve. Well, we thought she was very promising and that you'd all like to hear her again. So would you all give a big welcome, please, to Maura Reilly!"

May and Richie and Whacker clutched each other in excitement as everyone looked across to the far side of the studio, where Maura was suddenly to be seen in front of black and silver curtains.

She was wearing a green dress the colour of

her eyes and her red-gold hair flamed under the studio lights. Suddenly May heard again the music she had listened to backstage at the Olympia, holding the suit of armour ready for Queen Maeve's quick-change into battle-dress. She felt the muscles in her throat tighten. Suppose, she thought, the introduction finished and no sound came from Maura's lips. Or suppose her voice shook, the way May felt her own would if she had to speak at this moment? But then she heard Maura's voice, strong and true, singing:

Cloth of purple, green and blue,
Cloth of brown and yellow too

"They should have had me and Mickser on afterwards to sing 'Maeve, Queen of Connacht'," Richie whispered, but May shushed him up quickly, noticing how the lights changed to a steely blue as Maura came to the last verse with its:

Sword of silver, sword of gold,
Keen, quick spear that's light to hold

Then May felt her own cheeks burning as the applause broke out all around her and

Maura bowed again and again until the lights went out on her,

"Maura Reilly, ladies and gentlemen!" Gaybo was saying, "and I think we're all going to hear a lot more of her before too long. But now we have someone who needs no introduction because he's been on our panel many, many times over the past twenty years." But, though they argued about whether a man should do the cooking while his wife went out to work and some woman talked about a book she had written on pony-trekking in the Himalayas, and Gaybo called out: "You can roll it there, Róisín", for a piece of film of a dolphin, May hardly heard them. She was thinking about Maura and how no-one would have guessed from the way she looked that, last night in the Square, she had clung on to May in terror at the thought of having to stand there on her own under the lights.

"Didn't you sing by yourself in the Olympia?" May had said, but Maura had only shaken her head.

"That was different. Then I was pretending to sing to Maeve and Ailill and they were there on the stage with me."

Now Gaybo was talking about her as if she

were going to be a star: Maura, who had shabby clothes because her father was unemployed and whom May always had to protect from Imelda's sharp tongue!

Only when Whacker was the first to guess that the unfinished jigsaw was a photo of the actor who played JR in Dallas did she come out of her trance in time to hear that he had won a micro-wave oven and to join in the general laughter at Gaybo's suggestion that now he could do the cooking while his wife went out to work. But, as Whacker said afterwards, "Can't I always flog it if Ma doesn't want it enough to give me anything for it?"

As they filed out of the studio at the end of the show, Maura met them in the passage. She had changed out of her green dress and looked the same as she did back home in the Square, except that her cheeks were still flushed with excitement.

"You were brill!" May cried, hugging her and, even though she was trying to behave like a star of stage and television, Maura found herself starting to jump up and down with May the way they always had if something exciting happened when they were small. Even the boys admitted she had been

good and Whacker in particular was thrilled
when she told him there were drinks going in
the hospitality room, because it was the last
programme before they rested the show for
the summer, and there would be minerals laid
on for them.

"Will there be sambos?" he asked. "I'm
starved with the hunger!" And of course there
were, and fishy things on little biscuits too,
though Whacker pointed out that they were
no good at all unless you took three at a go.

Even more exciting, Gaybo and all the
television people were there too and, when the
director came over to tell Maura he had been
very pleased with her, she introduced him to
the others. Whacker was still trying to think
of something really impressive to say, that
would make it clear that he was into television
and a technical man himself, when the
director turned away from him to whisper
something to Maura. She nodded quickly and,
as soon as he left, she turned to the others in
excitement.

"There's a new series starting soon," she
said, "and the producer saw me tonight and he
may have something in it for me."

"Some people have all the luck!" grumbled
Whacker, who had always been a great

success at parties in the Square, doing his Brendan Grace impersonations, but who had been turned down flat at the auditions for the Olympia.

"Are you going to go and see him?" asked Richie.

"He's on his way here now," Maura gasped. "He was in one of the other studios and saw me on the tomitor or something."

"You mean the monitor," Whacker corrected her importantly. "Like the one in the studio that we saw ourselves on."

"Are you talking about the goggle-box?" Richie asked, but Whacker shook his head.

"It's not a goggle-box, Redser", he explained. "It looks like a goggle-box only it's got no insides like a *real* goggle-box."

May was about to ask Whacker how he knew all these things when she saw a tall, fair-haired man coming towards them. His hazel eyes were fixed on Maura and he had such a nice friendly look that May felt sure he was a really nice person.

"I'm Michael Casey," he announced, smiling down at Maura. "How would you like to sing every week on my new light entertainment series?"

"Oh, I'd love it," Maura cried, but then an

awful thought suddenly struck her and she added, "only I have to go to school during the week. Would I have to be here before the evening?"

Michael Casey grinned.

"Not to worry," he said. "It's for the autumn schedule but we'll be taping it during the summer. We should be able to fit most of it into the school holidays. We may have to try to get you off one or two classes for the last couple of programmes, but we can worry about that in September."

Maura's insides felt like they did the time she had a go on the giant racer, with the way her hopes kept rising and falling.

"Would I get a real salary like in the Olympia?" she asked, "because I don't think Mammy'd let me do it otherwise."

"I take it you don't have an agent," he replied, laughing, "but I suppose Róisín has your address? She must have got it for your contract for tonight's show. I'll get Casting to write to you with all the details and you can talk it over with your mother and let us know."

Maura nodded.

"I'm sure it'll be O.K.," she said. "Just so long as it pays more than the contract cleaning."

"I think you may make your mind easy on that score," he reassured her seriously. "So we'll hope to see you then. And congratulations again on your spot tonight." Then he moved away across the room, his long stride bringing him through the crowd to the door in a couple of steps.

They all stood staring after him in silence while the noise of the party went on all around them. Whacker realised he had let a second television director go by without a word, while Maura seemed dazed at her sudden good fortune. May was the first to speak and all she said was: "Wow!"

The flush on Maura's cheeks deepened a little.

"He's real cool!" she agreed.

Richie gave them a quick glance of irritation. As sisters go, May wasn't the worst. He hoped she wasn't going to start carrying on like some of the ones he had noticed giggling in the chipper.

May noticed the look and glared at him. Then a voice from behind them suddenly broke into their thoughts. It was a deep rasping voice and May recognised it immediately because she had heard it more than once already that evening. It belonged to the man with the ear-phones. Glancing round, she saw that he was standing in the centre of a small group of men over at the drinks table.

"There goes the new producer," he said, and it struck May at once that there was something nasty about the way he said it. She turned to ask Maura about him, but Maura silenced her with a movement of her hand. She was obviously listening to the conversation too.

"Never mind, Jacko," a fat man was saying. "You're at the top of the panel for the next vacancy."

"If and when there is one," the man he called Jacko rasped. "There's not a single producer/ director within an ass's bawl of retiring age. I wouldn't mind but it was always me Theo wanted for his big shows."

"You always seem to be scheduled on all the Light Entertainment Specials right enough," a man wearing glasses agreed.

"And that's no coincidence," Jacko told him. "He rings the Senior Floor Manager and asks for me every time. Did you ever know him to go looking for Michael Casey?"

The men around him all shook their heads.

"Of course you didn't. But when Theo's on the interview board for the new producer/

director's job, it's a different story. I tell you, I
don't know what influence Michael Casey has,
but he must have an arm and a leg of someone
to get the job over my head, considering he's
spent most of his time in Studio Three on talks
programmes."

"Mind you, Michael Casey's O.K.," the fat
man argued. "I always like being on a crew
with him."

"All the same," the man with glasses said,
"he'll have his work cut out for him going
straight off a training course on to a Light
Entertainment series. He's not much
experience in that area."

"So what does he do?" Jacko banged his
empty glass down on the table angrily. "He
asks for me as Floor Manager. He gets the job
over my head and then I'm supposed to pull
the chestnuts out of the fire for him!"

"You can only do so much from the floor,"
the man with the glasses pointed out. "If he
gets himself into a mess in the box there's not
a whole lot you can do for him."

"Hasn't he got Bea as his Production
Assistant?" Jacko snapped back. "She'll hold
his hand for him in the box ."

The fat man nodded.

"A good P.A.'s half the battle, right enough,"

he agreed. "It wouldn't be the first time an experienced P.A. had virtually directed the show for a new boy."

"Oh, she could if she wanted to," the man with glasses agreed, "but she might just go by the book. If she only types in the shots he gives her and calls them out on the day it won't get him far."

"Did you never see the way she looks at him?" It was Jacko's voice again. "Bea will cover up for him in the box all right, and I'll be expected to do the same on the floor."

"It's tough sure enough," the fat man agreed, "but there's not much you can do about it."

"Isn't there though?" Jacko replied, and again May noticed that unpleasant smile. "There's more than one way of killing a cat, you know! Before the series ends Theo may be sorry he chose to promote Michael Casey rather than me."

"So what?" the fat man said. "Michael has the job all the same."

Jacko poured himself another drink.

"There's nothing done that can't be undone," he said.

The man with glasses shook his head doubtfully.

"It doesn't do to make enemies in this game," he said, "and Michael's the man who'll be putting in the report if anything goes wrong."

"Ah, but you've forgotten one thing." Jacko took a gulp from the glass in his hand before continuing and when he spoke again there was a note in his voice that made May shiver. "What goes up must come down and the higher the rise, the greater the fall." Then he seemed suddenly to notice that the young people had fallen unnaturally silent because he took a step away from them muttering, "Little pitchers have long ears!"

The others followed his backward glance and began to talk more quietly, so May could no longer hear what they said. She gripped Maura's arm.

"Did you hear?" she whispered.

"I couldn't understand the half of it," Maura whispered back.

"The fella with the walkie-talkie means to make trouble for Mr Casey somehow," May said. "I know that much. You'd better warn him."

"He'd think I was bonkers!" Maura gasped in horror. "And we'd no business ear-wigging in the first place."

"Maybe so, but something awful's going to happen him if you don't. Walkie-Talkie sounds like he means business."

"Maybe it's only the drink talking," Richie suggested.

"Walkie-Talkie's not stocious," May said flatly, "but he's like JR. He'd do anything. He gives me the shakes. You've got to do something, Maura."

"But I can't!"

"It's a dodgy one," Whacker agreed. "She doesn't want to go getting up anyone's nose and she only a wet day in the place."

"Don't you see, May?" Maura pleaded, "this is my big chance!"

"And that's why you've got to do something," May said. "Don't you see? It's not only for Mr Casey. If old Walkie-Talkie starts trick-acting he's going to bust up your show!"

2

Widen to Include Group

hen Maura turned up at the Leeson Hall for her first rehearsal, May's words and the conversation they had overheard were a long way from her mind. She was far too concerned with her own problems for she had woken that morning with a sore throat and suspected she might be starting a summer cold. Between fear of that making her voice husky and her conviction that all the others in the hall were confident and experienced professionals only waiting to laugh at her own inexperience, she had no time to worry about Michael Casey.

She saw him the moment she walked in the door, for his height made him easy to pick out. He was talking to a young woman who was marking out lines on the floor with white sticky tape. She had expected to see Walkie-

Talkie, for he had said he was to be on the show, but she could see no sign of him. Everyone else seemed to know each other and were chatting in groups beside the row of chairs over against the wall or around the piano.

As she hesitated by the door, she suddenly heard her name called. Swinging round, she saw that a man had come in the door behind her and was delighted to recognise someone she knew. It was the actor who had played the part of Ailill in the Olympia show.

"Roger!" she cried. "What are you doing here?"

"Same as yourself, I imagine," he replied. "So you're in this little number too, are you? I can't say I'm surprised. I saw you on *The Late Late Show* and decided our little Maura was on her way."

Maura flushed, but she was glad he was there. He was not the sort of person she could ever like a lot, but he had always been kind to her and it gave her one person at least to talk to amongst all these strangers.

"What do we do now?" she asked. "I mean, I've only ever sung the one song on a show and I wasn't asked to bring music or anything."

Roger shrugged.

"I know no more about it than you do," he said. "I suppose the producer will tell us when he's good and ready."

Just then Michael Casey turned away from the girl with the sticky tape and looked around the hall. Then he clapped his hands together to get everyone's attention.

"Right, folks," he said, crossing over to the piano. "Gather round, will you, and I'll try to give you an idea of what this is all about."

By the time they broke for lunch, Maura's head was in a whirl. It seemed that each of the thirteen shows in the series would have a theme and the songs, dances and sketches in the show would all fit into this theme. The show had a researcher and script-writer to provide the rough story-line and sketches, a musical director and arranger for the music and a choreographer to devise the dances. Each week they would have to go to the Wardrobe Department at the Studios to sort out what costumes could be adapted for them and what would need to be specially made. She would only be singing two songs in each show, but one of them would be in a production number in which the whole cast would be involved. It would be like a mini-musical and her song would be part of the story. She would also be expected to take part in some of the sketches, though she might only have a few words to say.

"You might be the hat-check girl or a waitress in a night-club scene using the dancers or something like that," Michael Casey explained to her. "You wouldn't have more than a line or two of dialogue to learn, but I want everyone in the production numbers and I want to use singers and dancers to build the sketches, though they will be mainly for Sylvia and Roger."

"Sylvia!" gasped Maura. "Do you mean Sylvia Desmond?", for she had played Queen Maeve.

Michael Casey laughed.

"There's only one Sylvia in show-business in this country," he said. "She'll be here this afternoon. I let her off this morning because she went and got herself married yesterday and she already knows all the things I'm telling you now. You see, she's become Mrs Theo Sylvester, wife of our esteemed Head of Light Entertainment."

Maura heard a gasp from Roger and was surprised by the look on his face. There was no mistaking the fact that the news did not please him.

"Well," he exclaimed, "she certainly managed to keep that quiet! I did a radio commercial with her last week and she never said a word about it!"

Maura found it hard to believe that Roger could show so much feeling about anything Sylvia would do, as long as it did not cut one of his lines or force him to turn his back on the audience. He certainly could not be jealous of Sylvia's new husband. During the show in the Olympia, she had decided that he was really only interested in himself and his career.

"A clever move, all the same," he continued. "If there's any work going in Light Entertainment from now on, you can be sure the boss's wife will get it!"

That explained everything, Maura thought. It was Sylvia herself he was jealous of! But she forgot all about Roger too in the discussion over what she should sing in the first programme, which was to be on the theme of emigration. The dancers were to be emigrants and there would be scenes from John B Keane's *Many Young Men of Twenty* and James McKenna's rock-and-roll musical *The Scatterin'*. Maura had seen neither of them and when she heard this she started to panic. Suppose they just handed her a sheet of music and expected her to be able to sing the air straight away. She would have to explain in front of the whole cast that she had never learned to read music.

Michael explained that Sylvia would be singing the title number from *Many Young Men of Twenty* while Roger would do some fifties rock numbers on his own and with the dancers. Maura could not picture herself doing anything like that. They would have done better to have used Whacker, she thought. Rock was right up his street, that and break dancing. Then she heard her own name.

"Maura will be a young emigrant on the Holyhead boat, because I want this brought up to date. When the musicals were written it was mainly the men leaving the country but today it's the girls as well. I see her singing a very simple number, a song that would say something about the heartbreak of having to leave home. Any ideas, Maura?"

Maura felt the colour rising in her cheeks. They were all looking at her, waiting for her to say something. Wasn't "Danny Boy" about emigration? She had sung that at her audition in the Olympia. Then she remembered the party thay had had in the

Square a year ago when Liz Meany from No. 42 had had to go to England to look for work. Everyone had sung noisy songs until it was time for Liz herself to sing. She had stood up, slowly, and started to sing "Molly Malone", standing very still and, as she sang, the tears began to trickle down her face until Maura, who had never liked Liz very much, thinking her a bit of a show-off, suddenly wanted to put her arms around her and tell her to be sure and come home again soon.

"I could sing 'Molly Malone'," she said. "Or 'Danny Boy'."

"'Molly Malone' was rather done to death during the Dublin Millenium," Michael said, "but it would depend on what you did with it. 'Danny Boy' is a bit over-used too, but they're both the sort of song someone might sing in the circumstances. You can sing them both for me this evening and we'll decide then. For your second number I want something that's not Irish. D'you know that Judy Garland number, 'Over the Rainbow'?"

"I don't know all the words," Maura stammered, "but I could soon learn them. I know the air."

"Good," Michael said and then, raising his voice, "Now we'll have Sylvia from two o'clock and Jack Olden and the Sound and Lighting people will be dropping in to find out exactly what we're at and if it gives them any problems. Bea!"

Maura had already noticed the slim fair-haired girl, because she had a stop watch hung around her neck on a cord and she seemed to follow Michael everywhere, her arms full of scripts and sheet-music. Now she appeared immediately at his side.

"For anyone who doesn't already know, this is Beatrice Carr, my production assistant," Michael Casey said. "She'll be giving you your scripts, rehearsal schedules and calls for Wardrobe and finding out where you can be contacted. When you've seen her, everyone but Roger and the dancers can go, but be back here on the dot of two o' clock."

Then he had turned away and begun talking to a man at the piano. Maura, finding herself right beside the girl he had called Bea, said: "Will I give you my address now?"

Bea, her eyes still on Michael as he crossed the hall, sighed and turned to Maura, flipping back a page on her clipboard.

"Go ahead," she said.

Maura gave her the number of their house in the Square, though she thought it was silly because they had already written to her there.

"Telephone number?" Bea questioned, her pencil poised above the clipboard.

"We don't have a telephone," Maura admitted, feeling foolish.

"So where do we contact you in a hurry?", Bea asked.

"Maybe at Flynn's," Maura said. "My Dad's there most evenings and they'd probably send Willie Doyle over with a message if you said it was urgent."

"D'you have that number?"

Maura shook her head. "It's in the book, though. Flynn's pub on Ormond Quay."

"Right," Bea said. "Here's your script, though a lot of it's only rough so far, so don't panic. Michael will go through it all with you this evening. Can you go to Wardrobe tomorrow morning?"

"Haven't I to be here?" Maura asked. "I thought I'd be rehearsing every day?"

"Yes, but we won't need everyone all the time. We could manage without you for an hour or so. Why don't you go about twelve and then you could get your lunch in the canteen before coming back here at two?"

"O.K.," Maura said. She expected there would be nothing in the canteen she could

afford to buy. It would be cheaper to bring
sandwiches like she had done today, but there
was no need to tell Bea that, so she just asked:

"What do I say to them in Wardrobe?"

"Tell them who you are, that's all. They'll
take your measurements. I'll give them a list
of what you'll need. They may have something
suitable from some other show that you could
try on. If not, they'll make something, and I'll
let you know if they want you again for a
fitting."

"O.K.," Maura said. It was silly to be edgy
about it. They had given her a dress in
Wardrobe when she had nothing of her own
that was nice enough for *The Late Late Show*.
It was really the same as the Wardrobe on the
top floor of the Olympia Theatre, where May
had spent weeks pressing tunics for the
musical. But this time there would be no May,
and no Richie, Imelda or Mickser either. It
had helped to take her mind off her stage-
fright, having them in the chorus, trick-acting
at rehearsal and before the show. She had had
to do *The Late Late Show* on her own, but at
least she was singing the number she had
sung every night for weeks in the Olympia.
Now it would be like having a first night every
week all through the summer.

It was such a lovely sunny day that she thought she would eat her sandwiches by the canal so, leaving her bike at the hall, she crossed the churchyard and walked towards Leeson Street Bridge. There were cars passing up and down the canal road in a steady stream, but she found a spot by the water's edge, where the grassy bank shielded her from the noise and smell of car exhausts. A pair of swans glided up from the direction of Baggot Street and she began throwing them the crusts from her sandwiches. The water creamed back like the wake of a ship each time the cob surged forward to grab a crust and his neck arched gracefully as he raised it from the water.

Watching the swans calmed her until she was able to read right through the script Bea had given her without the nervous feeling she had had in her stomach every time she thought about it. It sounded interesting and she had very few lines to say, just as Michael had promised. She suddenly realised she had not got a cold after all. It must have been nerves that had made her throat sore and her head ache.

She read the script through twice and then wondered what the time was. She had noticed a clock on the big building beyond the canal, but the wall it was on ran at an angle so she could not read the time from where she sat. The swans, giving up hope of getting anything more to eat, had drifted away. Maura put the empty sandwich bag into a blue rubbish bin nearby and walked to the bridge to see the time. It was only half-one, but there was nowhere else to go, so she walked slowly back to the rehearsal hall.

When she got there the outside door off the quandrangle was open, but the door of the hall itself was locked, so she sat on a seat in the passage outside. Then she heard a voice coming from the far end of the passage.

"It's just for the production number," the voice said, and Maura recognized it as that of Bea Carr, Michael's production assistant. "Michael wants three or four really young people on the boat. Not the usual extras you send over. They've to look like drop-outs from school. No, no. Not nearly young enough. Well, in that case, I suppose Equity wouldn't mind if we got someone to bring in their kid brother or something? Right."

Maura heard the jangle of the phone cutting out, as Bea came out of a door looking harrassed and scribbling a note on her clipboard.

"You're back early," she said when she saw Maura and then, suddenly: "You don't by any chance have any brothers and sisters, do you?"

Maura saw her chance. Maybe the series could be as much fun as the Olympia after all.

"No," she said quickly, "but I've friends who are as good as."

"What sort of age?" Bea asked.

"May Byrne's the same age as me and her brother Richie's a year older. And then there's Imelda and Whacker Kelly—they're the same age as May and Richie..."

"Imelda and Who Kelly?" Bea queried, her biro suspended in mid-air.

"His name's Paddy but we call him Whacker," Maura explained. "And then there's Mickser Dolan..."

"Stop!" gasped Bea. "That's more than enough! I only need three or four."

"That's our gang," Maura explained. "The others were all in the Olympia with me, except for Whacker, but he's the best of all of us at rock and..."

"O.K., O.K. They haven't to do anything but dress the set. I'll tell Michael you can lay on five and we'll see how many he wants. Are they on the phone?"

"Same as for me," Maura said. "Their Da's all drink in Flynn's too."

"It must do a good trade," Bea commented, taking a key from her pocket and unlocking the door of the rehearsal hall. "I can leave this open if you're going to be here. I'm just dashing across the road for a bite of something. If Michael gets back before me you can tell him I won't be five minutes."

But there was no need to tell Michael Casey anything. He was far too busy congratulating Sylvia, who arrived on the dot of two o'clock in a wave of blood-red nail varnish. She was immediately surrounded by a crowd of well-wishers, leaving Maura hovering shyly on the fringe. That was why she noticed that Roger, too, hung back and that Walkie-Talkie, arriving in the door in the midst of all the excitement, noticed the same thing.

"Now we know why Michael's directing this show!" he growled into Roger's ear. "Sylvia must have asked for him. Did you ever see a new bride kissing someone other than her husband with such enthusiasm?"

"Probably cupboard love," Roger growled back. "Michael's brother's tied in with that new film company. Sylvia always knew which side her bread was buttered."

Maura saw Walkie-Talkie's light-blue eyes brighten with interest.

"If Michael's wise, he'll play along," he rasped back. "It will do him no harm at all to push Theo's new wife!"

That was the worst thing he could have said to Roger, Maura decided. If Sylvia got one close-up more than he did, he would sulk over it. And Walkie-Talkie must know that too, she thought, as she watched him push his way into the crowd to offer his congratulations to Sylvia.

"Thanks, Jacko!" Sylvia said to him, kissing him too.

Sylvia's kisses meant nothing, Maura thought, remembering how she had kissed everyone at the party after the last performance in the Olympia. Sylvia was like that: always talking loudly and calling everyone "love" or "darling". Maura could see no difference between her manner with Michael and the way she treated everyone else.

Then Sylvia spotted Maura.

"Will yous look at who's here!" she commanded the whole room in the loud, exaggerated Dublin accent she always used when she was trying to prove there was nothing grand about her, even though she was the star. She ran over and enveloped Maura in a perfume-stifling hug. "D'yous know that this one played my devoted little maidservant for three whole months and not a whinge out of her! I should have had a proper white wedding," she went on, turning back to Maura, "with you as my bridesmaid to carry my train instead of my cloak!"

"I hope you'll be very happy, Sylvia," Maura whispered, her cheeks burning with the thought that everyone was looking at her.

Michael put a stop to the chatter then and the rehearsal started in earnest. Bea had given Maura the sheet music of "Over the Rainbow" but, since she knew the air, she had only to read the words written underneath the music notes. When her final "Why, then oh why, can't I?" died away, Sylvia broke into applause. It gave Maura a lovely feeling of confidence. Sylvia was generous and warm-hearted, she thought, so what did it matter that she was a bit theatrical and full of herself?

In the end, Michael had chosen "Danny Boy" for her second number, but Maura did not mind. All she had to do, she thought, was to sing "Danny Boy" the way Liz Meany had sung "Molly Malone": standing very still and wondering how long it would be before she saw everyone in the Square again.

Sylvia belted out her numbers, which were all as strong and dramatic as she was herself. Roger seemed fine on his own, too, but when he sang with Sylvia he watched Michael the whole time, trying to guess where the cameras would be. Michael blocked the production number so, as he said, "Jacko and the lads can get an idea of the thing," but he only cared where they all stood and not how they read their lines, so there was nothing for Maura to worry about.

"We'll be rehearsing this properly after lunch tomorrow," he told her, showing her how some of the white tapes she had seen the stage manager putting down on the floor that morning marked the deck of the Hollyhead boat.

By the time they broke rehearsal for the day, she was beginning to look forward to it all. The others were going across to the pub, to have a drink on Sylvia.

"Sorry I can't bring you," Sylvia said to Maura, "but get yourself and the gang a few minerals from me," and she tucked something into the pocket of Maura's cardigan.

"It will be minerals only for me too, I'm afraid," Michael said regretfully. "I've promised myself I'm going to stay on the dry until I have this series in the can."

"Are you mad?" Walkie-Talkie cried. "You can't offend Sylvia by refusing a drink. Don't you know she feels bad she never had a proper wedding reception?"

"She'll feel worse still if I make a bags of this show!" Michael said. "I'm going to need all my wits about me if I'm going to do a good job on it, so I'd better stay off the jar."

"Sure," Walkie-Talkie replied easily, "but one half-one just to wish Sylvia luck is hardly going on the jar."

"Maybe not," Michael said uncertainly, "but this series is a pretty big order for a fledgeling director, Jacko. That's why I'm relying on you for your support."

"Oh, you can count on me!" Walkie-Talkie called encouragingly, as Michael left with the others, but then added, under his breath, "to do all I can to louse things up."

He did not notice Maura, anxiously watching him as he ran off to join the others.

3

Mix to the Square

ext morning in Wardrobe, they found two dresses, a green and a brown one, both of which had been made for previous programmes but which would need only minor alterations to fit Maura as if they had been made for her. They took her measurements all the same, in case they needed to make something for a later programme in the series, so, by the time the dresses had been pinned, it was getting late. There would hardly be time to take her sandwiches to the canal bank when she got back to Leeson Street. Today would be a bad day to chance being late, she thought, for Michael Casey was in ill-humour. He had hardly had a word to throw to a dog all morning, and Maura hoped he would not be like that too often, for there were few in the

cast that had not felt the rough side of his
tongue. In the circumstances, she thought, it
would be best to go back right away to be sure
of being on time. She could eat her sandwiches
in the hall, so long as Bea had left the outer
door unlocked again.

"You know where the canteen is?" the
friendly assistant in Wardrobe asked, almost
as if she had been able to read Maura's
thoughts.

"It's all right. I've got sandwiches," Maura
told her.

"They don't like you to eat them in the
grounds," the assistant said. "They think it
makes RTE look like Dollymount Strand. Why
don't you take them to the canteen? You can
buy yourself a cup of tea or a coke and help
yourself to a plate and a knife for free. Sylvia's
due in at any moment and she can give you a
lift back to the hall when she's going."

"I wouldn't like to ask her," Maura
protested.

"She wouldn't mind. Sylvia's not like that.
I'll tell her you're in the canteen and want a
lift."

It all seemed to have been decided for her,
Maura thought, as she crossed the grass
between the studio and the canteen block and

pushed the revolving door into the vast room. She was bewildered by the babble of voices and the crowded tables scattered around the area, which was bounded on three sides by full-length windows so that the people looked like fish in an aquarium. While she hesitated, she saw a girl help herself to a can of coke from a cabinet near the door and carry it over to the check-out desk so she did the same. Then, when she had paid for it, she looked around for somewhere to sit.

Nearly all the tables were full, but there was one which three men were just leaving, so she took their place and began to unwrap her sandwiches. Then she remembered the plate and knife. It was not that she had any need of them, but their absence would draw attention to the fact that she had brought her own food with her and she was not sure whether that was allowed, so she hurried back to the counter. As she fished a knife out of the pile on the stand near the check-out, she heard a familiar rasping voice. Walkie-Talkie was seated nearby in one of the compartments formed by wooden partitions, surrounded by a group of men.

"I'll bet he had a sore head at rehearsal this morning," he was saying, with a harsh laugh.

"I'm glad I'm not Bea Carr."

So he was talking about *her* rehearsal! She delayed over the knife box, pretending to search around in it for a knife with a serrated edge.

"Theo won't be too pleased if he hears what happened," the fat man was saying. "It doesn't look good for RTE—the guards having to be sent for an' all."

Maura gave a little start. What on earth could have happened? When the guards turned up in the Square it invariably meant disaster of one kind or another for somebody. Now she had to stay and listen. If she went back to her table she would be out of earshot. But she did not want them to notice her earwigging. She saw a water-dispenser and glasses beside her and that seemed to provide an excuse. She took a glass and pressed it against the button so that the water began to trickle slowly into her glass from the little tap.

"Theo will be sure to hear all about it from Sylvia," another man was saying. "He has a spy in the camp now."

"Not at all," replied the Sound Operator, who had been at the rehearsal with Walkie-Talkie the day before. "Don't you think Sylvia knows it might damage Michael's chances?

She wouldn't want that to happen."

"You can take that as gospel," Walkie-Talkie said, with another unpleasant laugh. "She and Michael are thick as thieves and I hear she's angling for film work with the brother's company."

"All the same," the fat man argued, "Michael should have had more cop-on. It's one thing getting jarred like that at a party but it's quite another in a pub with his cast and crew."

So that was what had been wrong with Michael that morning, Maura thought. He had had a hangover. But that still did not explain why the guards had been called. You could see drunks leaving Flynns every night of the week, but no-one called the guards unless there was a fight or something.

A trickle of cold water on her hand reminded her that her glass was full to overflowing. She could stand there no longer without attracting attention. But as she walked back to her table, she heard Walkie-Talkie's rasping voice saying:

"Michael has a drink problem. If he as much as touches the stuff he's gone. You can forget about cop-on after that!"

Maura felt the blood surging into her cheeks

but this time it was with rage, not embarrassment. Walkie-Talkie had set Michael up! When he had insisted at the end of yesterday's rehearsal that Michael would offend Sylvia unless he had a half-one to drink her health, he had known he would be unable to stop at one. She was still thinking what a mean trick he had played when she saw Slyvia crossing the canteen towards her. She had forgotten, listening to Walkie-Talkie, that she was in a hurry. She gulped down her coke and stood up.

"I'm sorry to hurry you," Sylvia said, "but I don't want to be late back. Michael's in no humour for hanging around today."

"He looked the way my Dad does with a hangover," Maura said cautiously, trying to draw Sylvia into telling her the rest of the story.

"If you say that, or anything like it, to anyone else, I'll box your ears for you," Sylvia said sharply. "It's no business of yours."

"No, of course not. I'm sorry, Sylvia," Maura mumbled, but all the same she was glad. At least the Sound Operator had been right about that. Sylvia could be trusted not to give Michael away or let anyone else do so either.

Before that evening's rehearsal was over,

however, Maura had got the whole story, for
people hanging around awaiting their turn to
sing or dance have little else to do besides
gossip and the object of their gossip is more
than likely to be one of their own company.
Since they had all been in the pub at the time,
Sylvia would have her work cut out to shut
their mouths, Maura thought.

It seemed that Michael had got into a
drunken fight with Roger. It was odd because
all Roger had done, according to the story
Maura had managed to piece together from
the dancers' whispered gossip, had been to
suggest that Michael should go easy on the
drink when he had a rehearsal in the morning.
Maura remembered then how Walkie-Talkie's
words had aroused Roger's jealousy of Sylvia.
If Roger suspected Michael of favouring
Sylvia, there might have been something
nasty about the way he said it.

"What I don't understand," the little wispy
fair-haired dancer they called Dickie
whispered, "is who sent for the guards."

"The barman, I supposd," her friend Phyl
whispered back.

"It was not!" Dickie shook her plaits
vigorously. "I heard him complain the
landlord would be furious over them being

brought into it. He said he could have handled it himself."

"I doubt he could," Phyl argued. "Jacko had already done his best to stop them, before he had to go to the Gents to bathe his cut lip."

It was back to Walkie-Talkie again, Maura thought. And what was all this about a cut lip? She had been afraid to stare too hard at him in the canteen but she would surely have noticed if his lip had been swollen? A terrible suspicion began to form like a little cloud hanging over her head. She knew he had started Michael drinking. He could have set up the fight too, working on Roger's jealousy and Michael's drunken aggression. And then, well, he could have completed the set-up by ringing for the guards. She could almost see him, making a show of trying to part the two men while helping to egg them on and then, getting a slight blow on the face—or pretending to—and faking a cut lip. All he would have had to do would be to clap a hand over his mouth and mumble about going to bathe it. Instead, he could have slipped into the phone box and informed on Michael.

"Maura!"

Maura spun around. It was Michael coming towards her and her cheeks burned as if she was afraid he could have overheard her unspoken thoughts.

"Yes, Michael?" she said guiltily.

"Bea says you've friends who might do extra work," he said. "Would you ask them to drop in to rehearsal tomorrow so I can have a look at them?"

"All of them?" Maura asked stupidly, remembering that Bea had only wanted three or four.

"Bea mentioned five names to me," Michael said tersely. "I won't need them all but I'd like to pick the most suitable ones for myself."

"I'll bring them in with me tomorrow morning," Maura said.

"Fine!"

He had agreed with her suggestion and yet he had almost snapped out the word, instead of sounding pleased. As he turned on his heel, Maura thought he looked far from happy. But then, she had seen her father like that sometimes, the day after he had collected his dole money. Why on earth, she wondered, would anyone want to drink if it meant ending up like that, but she supposed that maybe they never thought that far ahead when they were singing their heads off in Flynn's.

She wished her father would stay out of

Flynn's. It caused such awful rows between him and her mother. At least Michael had plenty of money to waste on drink but at home they needed every penny. And yet, her father seemed to go to Flynn's more since he lost his job in the markets. Of course, he had so much more time now, unlike the days when he worked as a porter and had to start very early in the morning. She was still thinking about her father when she got back to the Square but, instead of going home, she called first to May and Richie's house.

"Hi!" said Richie, when he opened the door. "If you're looking for May, she ran across with the message for Danny Noonan."

Maura knew what that meant. The women in the Square took it in turns to do washing for the old sailor, who was too crippled with arthritis to do much for himself any more. May would be putting the little pile of freshly laundered clothes away in the press in his little house across the Square, while Danny told her tales of his many sea-voyages or things that happened in Dublin long ago in the days of the Vikings or when Ireland was under British rule.

"I want May and you too," Maura told Richie. "It's about doing extra work for RTE.

And they may want 'Melda and Whacker and Mickser too."

"Great!" said Richie. "Let's go and round up the gang."

Crossing the Square with Richie and Maura's dog Patchie at their heels, they bumped into Imelda on her way back from the shops. She was carrying a bulging plastic bag with a packet of cornflakes sticking out from the top.

"Will you come on down to old Danny Noonan's as soon as you've the messages left back?" Richie said, "and bring Whacker with you."

"I don't know will he come," Imelda said. He's watching some old science programme on the telly."

"He'll come on the double when he hears what it's about," Richie told her. "Just say there's a chance of being on the telly himself."

"I hope he doesn't get a let-down." Maura said anxiously, as Imelda sped on her way. "It's not for definite, you know. Michael mightn't pick Whacker. He'd be only mortified of he was the one left out again."

"Has he to sing?" Richie asked, remembering their auditions in the Olympia Theatre when Whacker had been stopped less than half-way through the comedy number he always got such applause for at parties in the Square.

"No-one has to do anything except walk around like they were on the deck of the Holyhead boat," Maura said, "but you'll get paid for the day and I won't be half as nervous with you all there."

"Don't you know well Whacker would do it for nothing to get the chance of a whole day in the studio," Richie said.

Maura knew Richie was right and hoped that, whoever was left out, it would not be Whacker. She knew that, while she would be thinking only of her performance and the others would be having a bit of gas, Whacker would be learning everything anyone could learn in a day. And if, by the end of it, he did not know everything there was to be known about the workings of a television camera and the duties of the floor manager and sound and lighting operators, no-one he talked to afterwards would ever for a moment suspect it. So Maura was not surprised that, by the time she and Richie had given the news to Mickser Dolan, Whacker and his sister had already arrived at Danny Noonan's door.

"Well, if it isn't the full ship's crew!" the old

sailor exclaimed, as they all crowded in after May into his little front parlour that was full of models of sailing ships inside bottles and old brass sextants and other souvenirs of his life at sea.

"You don't mind if they all come in, do you Danny?" May asked, holding Patchie by the collar so that he would not knock anything over in the crowded room.

"Where else would you go to chart a voyage?" he said, "And it's plain as a pint of porter that you're plotting some new course this minute. Where are you bound for this time, Captain?"

"We're hoping for work on the telly with Maura," Richie told him. "Go on, Maura. Tell us the deal."

So Maura told them about going with her to rehearsal next day, so Michael could pick three or four extras.

"I hope he picks me," May said. "I think he's lovely!"

"He wasn't lovely today," Maura told her. "He was in desperate humour. But I think that's maybe because he's scared."

"Isn't he the boss?" Imelda asked sharply. "I don't see what he has to be scared about!"

"It's that Walkie-Talkie," said May. "I just

know it is."

"You could be right," Richie agreed. "Didn't he threaten to make trouble the night Maura was on the *Late Late*?"

"He did," May said, "and I told Maura then she ought to warn Michael, but of course she funked it!"

"I couldn't," Maura said, "but I've wanted to since rehearsals began. I'm sure Walkie-Talkie set him up." And she told them everything that had happened.

"Tell me this and tell me no more," Danny Noonan said, when she had finished. "What has this Walkie fella got against your Michael?"

"He thought he should have got the job of director himself," Whacker explained, and told Danny the conversation they had overheard in the hospitality room.

"And now everything keeps going wrong," Maura added, "and Walkie-Talkie somehow always manages to make it look as if it's all Michael's fault."

"Of course," Richie said, "because he's hoping Michael will get the sack so as he'll get his job. I'll bet he planned the whole thing right from the start."

"He sounds a dead ringer for Iago," Danny

commented, "though precious good all his scheming did *him* in the heel of the reel!"

"A dead ringer for who, Danny?" May asked, puzzled.

"Iago. Did you never do any Shakespeare at that school of yours?"

"Oh, Shakespeare!" Mickser made a face. His glasses made him look like a swot, but it was May who always had her head stuck in a book. "We had to learn yards about some eejit in an ass's head, as well as a stupid song about fairies. Desperate stuff it was too!"

"That'd be *A Midsummer Night's Dream*," Danny told him, "but never let me catch you running down ould Willie Shakespeare. A grand storyteller he is and great value into the bargain. When my legs are that bad I can't be running in and out to the library every minute, there's nothing lasts longer than Shakespeare's *Collected Works* that has 37 plays and a pile of poems all bound together the way you can get them all out on the one ticket!"

"But what has Shakespeare to do with Michael Casey?" Maura asked.

"If you'd read him the way you should you'd know that he was the man could tell you all about the likes of the Walkie fella," Danny said, slipping into the tone he used whenever he was beginning one of his own stories. "He must have met many a quare hawk in his day, for he was a touring actor when theatre people were treated no better than robbers—and I daresay many of them were little better than robbers betimes, for they had mouths on them the same as anyone and if there was no audience for a play there'd be no money for food or rent. But Willie Shakespeare must have kept his eyes and ears well open to everything around him for I never met anyone could tell you more of the goings-on in the world, no matter if it was kings and queens and high-up persons in fine clothes or ordinary folk the same as you or me. For when Willie tells a story, whether it's about an old schemer like that fella on the telly with the cowboy hat and the cigar, or a class of a ghost story or a murder, you see right into the heart of the baddy as well as the good chap and get to know just how they're all thinking. And in one of his plays there's a baddy by the name of Iago and your Walkie fella sounds to me like his twin brother."

"What did this Iago fella do?" Richie asked.

"He was in the army and when another lad was promoted to Captain rather than himself, he used every sort of knavery and trickery to poison the mind of the General against him."

"And did he get the Captain's job?" Whacker asked.

"He did not," Danny said. "He was found out in the end and taken away to be tried for all his wrongdoings, but not before he had caused desperate mayhem that led to the deaths of two people, the General and his wife."

"Oh Danny!" Maura cried, "That's terrible! You don't think anyone could get killed over Walkie-Talkie, do you?"

"You never know," the old sailor said thoughtfully, "for when a ruthless and ambitious man sets about robbing someone of their good name, there's no knowing where it may all end!"

Two-Shot of Maura and Whacker

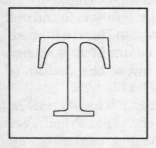

he following day, they all set out on their bikes for rehearsal. Patchie followed them, but he turned back at the bridge when Richie shouted at him to go home. It was a fine morning, and the sun sparkled on the waters of the Liffey.

They turned left off Parliament Street and took the short cut that led to the circle entrance of the Olympia Theatre, through what old Danny Noonan was always telling them had once been "a little gem of a square, may God forgive them that knocked it!"

May glanced at the theatre as they turned out of the little lane on to Dame Street at the side of the main foyer doors.

"I wish it was in there we were going," she said. "I never had so much fun."

"And we got a few bob for it in the heel of the

hunt," added Mickser, for whom this was always the most important thing.

"Telly pays better than the theatre," Whacker said, knowing all about this too.

"Yeah, but we'll only get a day or so out of it," Mickser argued. "It's not like we were getting taken on for the summer. A long-running show gives you more bread than a day's telly."

"If we were even sure of that!" Imelda added.

Maura said nothing. She just led the way up Georges Street, out through Exchequer Street and into William Street. Imelda looked longingly at the Powerscourt Shopping Centre. The clothes in there were only brill and they had super eats as well. If she got picked she might go shopping there some day. May glanced at Maura's back and noticed how her shoulders drooped dejectedly over the handlebars. She pedalled faster and caught up with her.

"What's wrong?" she asked quietly.

"Oh, just the Da!" Maura shook her head in irritation. "He seems mad at me about something. He says I'm getting above myself—putting on grand airs and that. 'The fillum star' he keeps calling me."

"He's only teasing," May said.

"He's not!" Maura shook her head again. "It was real snappy, the way he said it. And I've done nothing on him!"

"It must be awful for him being so long idle," May said. "I bet he feels bad about it. You having a job and he still on the dole. Did you never think of that?"

"No." Maura looked surprised. "I thought he'd be glad I was bringing money into the house."

"Of course he is. But he could be kind of jealous too. Don't mind him, Maura. Just think of being on the telly."

"That only makes me scared."

"That's stupid. I'd love to be you and to be able to sing. Only for them needing help in the Wardrobe I'd have got nothing in the Olympia, same as Whacker."

"Well, you haven't to sing this time. Oh, May, I really hope he picks you!"

"So do I," May said fervently, and the two of them rode on in silence.

As they chained their bikes to the pillars under the covered walkway outside the door of the hall, they could hear Roger singing one of his rock numbers.

"We must be late," Maura said anxiously,

breaking into a run. "They've started already."

But when she opened the inner door there was no one there but Roger. He was sitting at the piano, banging out the accompaniment for himself and he never even paused when they came in. Remembering them all from the Olympia, he just gave a half-turn of his head by way of greeting and kept on playing and singing.

They stood just inside the door for a few minutes listening. Then Whacker threw off his jacket and began breakdancing. Considering his stocky build he was remarkably good at it, and, as the dancers drifted in, they clustered around to watch, cheering him on.

Roger came to the end of the number, but Phyl called to him to keep going so he began pounding out a rag. Everyone was by now so absorbed in the action, as Whacker turned and turned on his hands, that it was only when Sylvia shouted that Maura realised that the room was full of people.

"Whacker, you're only brill!" she screamed. "You must do that in the show, mustn't he, Theo?"

Whacker collapsed, red-faced, on the floor, the sweat darkening the edge of his fair hair, as Maura turned to see a man she had never met before, standing beside Sylvia. He was a good bit older than any of the others, with greying hair and glasses.

"That's up to Michael," he said, smiling, "but it might be fun. It would at least show it's the here and now we're on about, even if we are using numbers out of the fifties. What d'you think, Michael?"

"Who is he?" Michael asked, pushing his way over, with Bea at his heels as usual.

"You asked me to bring him this morning," Maura explained anxiously.

"That's right," Bea confirmed. "He's one of your possible extras. And there should be four others for you to pick from."

"That's us," Richie announced, making a circling movement with one arm that included May, Mickser and Imelda.

Michael glanced at them briefly and then nodded to Bea.

"O.K." he said. "Four extras and a 'special.' We'll have the lot."

Maura forget again that she was a professional and hugged May, jumping up and down with her as they had always done when they were excited.

"Just like a couple of footballers after

scoring a goal," Roger commented, looking at them in disgust.

"We won't need you before studio," Michael said to Richie, whom he had already recognised as the leader of the group. "You can sign 'on the spot' contracts then. But if you want to stay and watch the rehearsal now you can, as long as you don't talk. Now," and he turned away from Richie to address the others, "quiet everybody, please!"

The buzz of conversation died down and everyone turned to face Michael. He in turn indicated the man with grey hair and glasses.

"This is Theo Sylvester, Head of Light Entertainment," he said. "He'll be watching rehearsal too, so you'd all better be good!"

"Hi, everybody!" the older man said casually, and he sat down beside the exhausted Whacker on the bench against the wall.

"Is that Sylvia's husband?" Maura whispered, aghast. Roger nodded.

"Did you notice the way she appealed to him over Michael's head?" he whispered back by way of reply. "She's getting above herself altogether now."

It was the very thing her father had said about her, Maura thought, and it was not true of Sylvia either. She had always been the same, saying right out what she thought, never stopping to wonder whether she might offend anybody. But Roger was jealous of her, so he saw her differently now. Maybe May had been right when she said Maura's father might be jealous of her. But all she whispered to Roger was "He's real old!" because that was what seemed strangest to her. Sylvia was so full of life, so loud and bouncy. How could she have chosen to marry this quiet grey man who looked old enough to be her father?

Waiting for the traffic lights to change in Dame Street on their way home from rehearsal, she said the same thing to May.

"She must be bonkers!" May agreed. "Imagine choosing him when she could have that dishy Michael!"

"Don't suppose she ever got a chance with Miss Stop Watch on guard all day!" Imelda sniffed.

"If you mean Bea, she's his assistant," Maura said. "It's her job to stay with him."

"I tell you she's nuts about him," Imelda argued. "I was watching her. She never took her eyes off Michael and the ould fella never took his eyes off Sylvia."

"That must be it so," May said. "Michael and

Sylvia never got a chance."

"Just because you fancy him you think everyone else must too," Whacker said. "Michael's cool all right, but Mr Sylvester's nicer."

"How d'ya know?" Richie asked. "He never opened his mouth."

"Maybe not to you," Whacker said grandly. "He asked me what I wanted to do when I left school!"

"And did you say you wanted to be a scientist?" Imelda asked.

"That was years ago," Whacker told his sister impatiently. "I told him I wanted to work in television."

"You didn't!" Maura looked at him wide-eyed.

"Why not? Wasn't it a chance in a million?"

"You mean, he might give you a job?"

"Maybe, one day. Anyway, he said if I liked I could sit in the director's box with him tomorrow and see how a show was put together."

"What show?"

"I dunno. Whatever's in studio tomorrow. Some light entertainment show, I suppose, if it's one of his. We're not wanted at rehearsal till the weekend so there's nothing to stop me."

Maura looked at him in amazement. It was extraordinary how Whacker made things happen. Things happened to her all right, but always by accident. She would never have got this job if Michael had not happened to see her on the *Late Late* and she would not have done that if Gaybo had not happened to see her at the Olympia.

"I told him I'd watched the crew in studio on the *Late Late*," Whacker went on, "but you couldn't really tell what was going on from there. And he said that was true, you'd need to see it from the box. Then he invited me for tomorrow."

Waiting next day while the dancers rehearsed on their own with the choreographer, Maura wondered how Whacker was getting on. They had left the Square together on their bikes that morning and parted near Leeson Street Bridge, as Whacker continued on to the television studios. He probably knew the names and life stories of the whole crew by now, she thought. She wished she was able to make friends as easily. Even now, she hesitiated to join in the chatter of Phyl, Dickie and the others.

Then Sylvia arrived and Maura felt sure that something was wrong. The skin around her smudgy eyes was puffy and pink, as if she might had been crying and, instead of bouncing over to greet everyone, she slipped into the corner by the piano and pretended to study her script. Maura knew she must be pretending because she never turned the pages but kept staring at the same pages without moving. But it was when Michael appeared that Maura knew for certain that there was trouble. His face had a greyish tinge and he snapped at Bea as she fussed around him with anxious glances. The rehearsal went badly and Maura was glad when Bea told her they were finished with her for the day.

"There's no need to hang on here," Bea said, "but will you call out to Wardrobe before you go home? They just want to check that the alterations are O.K." Then she added, "But if you want to hang on we'll be going out there ourselves later."

Catching a glimpse of Michael's face, Maura was glad she had her bike. Maybe Whacker would have seen enough in the studio by the time she was finished and they would be able to go home together.

* * * * *

Whacker had enjoyed himself thoroughly, watching the banks of monitors behind the control desk, as they recorded a quiz programme. It was true that Mr Sylvester had not been as helpful as Whacker had hoped. He seemed to be in ill-humour and sat silent in the control room, speaking only when someone asked him a question. He had, however, introduced Whacker to the director and his assistant, the designer and the vision mixer, who sat facing a row of knobs and switches on the control panel. It was she who had explained to him how the picture Camera One was shooting could be seen on the first monitor and Camera Two's and Three's pictures on the second and third, while the one the director had chosen to record would be repeated on the fourth. She showed him how she could cut quickly from one picture to another or mix them so that one picture gradually faded down and another came through it in its place. She explained how the sound was being recorded in the room on the far side of the glass panel behind them and the lighting done from the room next door and, while they waited for the audience to be seated, she took him through the door in the glass panel beside them on to the gallery, from where they could look down on to the studio below.

"That's the Floor Manager," she told him. "The one wearing the cans," and at once Whacker recognised the angular figure of Walkie-Talkie. He was to hear his voice, crackling over the microphone, all day, and soon realised how important he was to the show.

"Jacko!" the director would call into his microphone, "can you have a quiet word with our question master and tell him to slow down a bit? If he goes on at that rate, no one's going to hear a word he says and we'll run out of questions before we're through."

"Right, Gov," the speaker would crackle back in Walkie-Talkie's voice, or perhaps he would appear on one of the monitors, giving a thumbs up sign into the camera. And if there were delays over lighting or getting a contestant into position, the director would call, "Jacko! What's the problem?" or "Hurry them up Jacko, please!"

For the rest of the day, Whacker noted how Walkie-Talkie was the link between the director in the control room and everything that happened in the studio. He has the power to make or break a show, Whacker thought, and decided there and then that what he really wanted to be was a Floor Manager.

They were doing two programmes "back to back" as the director put it—one in the morning and the other after the lunch break—and, as they were breaking for lunch, Whacker saw through the glass panel beside them Walkie-Talkie's head suddenly appear over the edge of the gallery as he came up the ladder-like stairs leading from the studio.

"Are you happy with that one?" he asked the director.

Satisfied with the grunted reply, he turned to Theo Sylvester.

"How about you, boss? You happy too?"

Theo nodded, but Jacko went closer, studying him with eyes that missed nothing.

"You don't look it," he went on. "What's wrong?"

"Nothing!" Theo said shortly. "The programme's fine."

As the others stood up, stretching, collecting their belongings and chattering as they left the control room, Jacko lowered his voice so that Whacker had to strain his ears to catch what he said.

"Don't be too hard on Michael," he said. "Roger was really asking for it."

"And when I want your advice, *I'll* ask for it," Theo replied coldly.

"Fair enough, boss!" Jacko did not seem in the least put out. "But I don't like to see you upsetting yourself about something that's over and done with. I'm sure Michael will watch it in future. He knows he has a drinking problem."

Whacker saw Theo stiffen to attention.

"Has he?" he asked.

"I'm sorry!" Jacko mumbled, appearing embarrassed. "I thought you knew. But he's dead careful never to drink when he's a show to do. He just didn't like to refuse Sylvia on account of the day that was in it. He's very fond of her, you know." He broke off abruptly then, as if afraid he had said too much.

Theo's face darkened and, without a word, he left the control room. Whacker pretended to be studying the script the Vision Mixer had left lying on the desk, but he felt Walkie-Tallkie's sharp eyes on him as he too left the room.

"Are you coming over to the canteen?" one of the men called through the Sound Control Room, but Whacker said, "It's O.K., thanks. I've got sambos."

Walkie-Talkie had been going to the

canteen and he was better off away from his quick, suspicious glance. Besides, he wanted to think. It was surely the fight in the pub Walkie-Talkie had been discussing? And Maura had said last night she thought he had set that up. Now he was making sure Theo knew all about it. Or had he already known? And was that what had him in such bad form? Walkie-Talkie seemed to think so. But what he had said, though it sounded reassuring, had made Theo feel worse, not better. And Whacker felt pretty sure that was just what it had been meant to do.

Thoughtfully, he unwrapped his sandwiches, using the wrapping paper as a plate and taking care not to leave crumbs on the control panel, but, an hour later when the others returned from the canteen, he still had not figured out the exact meaning of what he had overheard.

Maura had tried on the dresses. Looking at herself in the long mirror before she took off the brown one she suddenly had a shivery feeling. Could this no-hoper who had to go to England to look for work really be her? More than half the girls who had left their school at the end of last term had already taken the boat. In another few years she could be doing the same. She would rather do that than join her father every week in the dole queue. And she was not clever like May, who was always first with the answers in class—nor as good with her hands. If there were any jobs going in either the Eastern Health Board office or the electronics factory May would be sure to get one. May would speak up at an interview, not stand silent and tongue-tied with burning cheeks the way she did herself.

It was only when she sang that she forgot the people looking at her and thought only of the song. But it had been the same with the production numbers. Even when she only spoke it was all right so long as she was playing a part and could feel it was not her at all, but the girl in the story that was speaking.

She had been scared the first time she had had to read her lines, expecting to feel awkward, but it had been fine. Once you had a script, you knew what to say. All you had to do then was learn the words. It was not like having to stand in front of someone, answering questions out of your own head. If she could only get work as a singer and an actress she would not have to go abroad looking for work. But then, as Mickser had said, a job on the telly did not last for very long. It was all right at the moment, when she only needed something for the holidays, but would she ever be able to earn a living at it?

The only hope, she thought, was that someone would see her in one show and offer her another, the way Gaybo had done and then Michael. But that meant that everything she did had to be good. She could not afford to make any mistakes. It was frightening to think like that and she shivered a little as she took off the brown dress and gave it back to the Wardrobe assistant. Thinking just how important this show was to be to her, she went to see if they were nearly finished in Studio One.

As she pushed open the door into the passage that linked the downstairs studios she heard footsteps and then Michael's voice.

"Please, Sylvia!" he was begging. "You're the only one who can help now. He won't listen to me!"

Maura froze, one hand still holding the swing door a little ajar.

"I tried, this morning." It was Sylvia speaking now. She must be passing close by on the other side of the door, Maura thought, because she was speaking quite softly. "He got really angry. Told me not to interfere. It's the first time he ever bit the head off me."

Maura heard Sylvia's high heels clacking away down the passage so, after a minute, she pushed the door open and peered cautiously round it. The passage was empty. She pushed open the second door and went into Studio One.

It was just like pushing open the door to the Olympia stage, Maura thought, because you could see nothing but the black drapes screening the entrance. Just as in the Olympia, you found yourself behind the set with only your ears to tell you whether it was empty or full of action. And your ears could deceive you because, if the Floor Manager had just shouted "Quiet, please!" twenty or thirty people could be silently grouped in front of the set or standing, hushed behind the cameras and sound booms.

So, although everything seemed silent, she crept quietly around the black drapes until she could see the whole studio. The audience had gone and the bleachers with their rows of seats deserted. The show must have only just finished, though, for a few of the crew were still around, coiling cables, and the last of the big floods went out as she arrived, leaving the studio lit only by working lights.

A sudden movement caught her eye and she saw it was Walkie-Talkie, on the stairs going up to the gallery. He was moving fast, running almost, but soundlessly on rubber soles, as stealthy as a cat. Then she saw Michael and Sylvia. They were on the far side of the bleachers, close to the sound boom on its little wheeled platform.

"He'll still be up there now if you hurry," she heard Michael say, noticing the urgency in his voice.

"Of course. He's waiting for me."

"Then you could talk to him. He might be in better humour now. If you can just get him to listen to me. I can't work with all this hanging over me. It's affecting the show!"

"Don't I know it? I don't want to be left with egg on my face either, you know, but I'm afraid of making things worse. I've never seen Theo like he was this morning."

"But we can't go on like this. It's destroying both of us!"

"I know, love, but I can't face Theo at the moment."

"Please, Sylvia! Without you, I'm lost!"

"Don't! I care just as much as you do you know."

"Then talk to Theo, please!"

"All right." Sylvia squared her shoulders. I'll try!" and she crossed the studio in the direction of the gallery stairs.

Whacker would be gone unless she hurried, Maura thought, but it was out of the question to go the way Sylvia had gone. How could she pass Michael, lounging moodily by the sound boom, his eyes on Sylvia as she climbed the steep, narrow stairway? She slipped quietly back the way she had come, crossed the reception area and hurried up the big, curving marble staircase.

When she was on the *Late Late Show* she had found out how you could get to the control room without going through the studio at all and now she raced along the corridors to get there before Whacker could leave. The place was such a maze, she thought, if she once missed him in the control room she would never catch him.

The door of the sound control room was open as she passed and she caught a glimpse of Walkie-Talkie, bent low over the sound panel. She wondered for a second what he was doing but the scene on the other side of the glass panel drove all thought of him from her mind. Whacker was nowhere to be seen, but Sylvia lay on the floor in a crumpled heap

sobbing, while Theo sat with his back to her at
the control desk, his head in his hands. Then
Maura felt a painful grip on both shoulders as
two hands yanked her viciously around,
forcing her along the narow passage.

"Get to hell out of here!" rasped a voice she
recognised immediately.

"What's wrong?" she protested. "I was only
looking for Whacker."

"I don't care who you were loooking for,"
Walkie-Talkie growled. "You've no business
here. No-one sets foot in studio without
permission from the Floor Manager and that's
me. Did I give you permission?"

"No, Jacko," Maura stammered, "but I'm not
in the studio!"

"You were just now. I saw you snooping
around down there. Your show doesn't come
into studio until next weekend, *if* you're still
in it."

"What do you mean, if I'm still in it?"
Maura's hands were shaking now, but she
stood her ground.

"I'm just warning you, that's all. Nobody is
indispensable!"

"B-but...I've a contract   for the whole
series!"

"Then you'd better read the small print. The

contract is broken if you don't keep studio discipline."

Maura looked at him aghast.

"What does that mean?"

"It means you'd better do as you're told and when you're in studio I'm the one that does the telling. You can't even talk to the director except through me! If you're a smart girl you'll see what side your bread is buttered. D'you get the message?"

Maura tried to speak, but something seemed to have happpened to her voice. She nodded instead.

"Well, I'd remember that if I were you. Because if I wanted to make trouble for you, you'd never even know what hit you!"

5

Track in on Walkie-Talkie

aura stood outside
the control room of
Studio One, her heart
hammering. What could have happened
between Sylvia and her husband in those
minutes it had taken her to run up from the
studio floor?

The brief glimpse she had of them before
Walkie-Talkie had flung her out had
reminded her of something she had tried to
forget. She heard again the street door
slamming shut behind her father as he
stormed across the square to Flynn's, saw
again the little trickle of blood as her mother
took her hand away from her face. She had
known what that was about. Her mother had
asked her father for extra out of his dole
money, telling him for the first time that she
had got herself deep in debt and that Ma

74

Sullivan, the money-lender was beginning to get nasty. Nothing like that could have happened with Sylvia and Theo, though. Maura thought they must be nearly millionaires, because they each had their own car and so many clothes that they must surely have an enormous house to have room for them all.

Whatever it was, she was certain Walkie-Talkie must come into it somehow. Suddenly she remembered what old Danny Noonan had said about the fellow in the play: "When a ruthless and ambitious man sets about robbing someone of their good name, there's no knowing where it may all end!" Walkie-Talkie would think nothing of wrecking Sylvia's marriage if it helped him to get Michael's job, or of wrecking the show that was so important to Maura. And he had made it clear that if she tried to interfere he could have her sacked.

Then, for the second time, she felt herself gripped by the shoulder as a hand covered her mouth, stifling the scream that burned in her throat. Too surprised even to struggle, she found herself yanked backwards through a door which closed behind her. While she was still held and gagged, she heard a voice warning her to be quiet. She let out a sob of relief, for it was a voice she knew well. She pushed aside the hand and turned to find herself in the Lighting Control Room facing no one more dangerous than Whacker.

"What did you do that for?" she demanded indignantly. "You scared the wits out of me!"

"Sh!" Whacker whispered urgently. "You don't want Walkie-Talkie to hear you."

Maura looked around her in surprise. The room she was in looked just like the Production Control Room only back to front, with the control panel and the banks of monitors facing the other way. Apart from Whacker and herself, the room was empty. How could Walkie-Talkie possibly hear them?

"He's playing around with the sound," Whacker explained. "By opening mikes he can hear what's happening everywhere."

Suddenly Maura knew what he had been up to in the Sound Control Room, but she still could not understand why. Whacker saw the puzzled look on her face.

"It was awful!" he whispered. "He opened the mike on the floor when Michael and Sylvia were talking and Theo heard everything they said."

Maura remembered they had been standing

close to the sound boom, but she still did not understand.

"Why was it awful?" she asked, keeping her voice low. "I was in studio too. They didn't say anything much."

"Didn't Sylvia as good as say it was Michael she wanted, not Theo?"

Maura stared at him in amazement.

"Not at all!" she said.

"But I heard her myself! Michael said he'd be lost without her and she said she cared as much as he did! And Michael said they couldn't go on like that and she'd have to tell Theo."

"Not at all!" Maura said again and then, lowering her voice as Whacker put a warning finger to his lips, "They were talking about the row in the pub. when the fuzz was called. It wasn't really Michael's fault but Theo won't let him explain."

"It didn't sound like that to me."

"Because you didn't hear what they said before. Michael asked Sylvia to talk to Theo because he's afraid Theo's going to take him off the show."

"If that's all it was about, why did Michael say it was destroying them both?"

"Because it is, and me too. Rehearsals are

desperate now. How would you like to get your big chance and then have everything go all wrong? Michael thinks someone else may be told to take over the show at any minute and that makes him even more nervous than he was before, on his very first programme as a director. And if Michael makes a mess of things it's Sylvia and me and the rest of the cast that will look stupid when the programme goes out!"

Whacker shook his head.

"It didn't sound like that," he repeated.

"Of course it didn't!" Maura understood it all now and she was so angry she forgot to whisper. "Walkie-Talkie made sure of that. He only opened the mikes when they were saying something he knew Theo would misunderstand.

They heard a door slam close by and feet pounding along the passage.

"Run!" Whacker shouted, flinging open the door on to the gallery, and Maura raced after him just as Walkie-Talkie burst in from the passage. As she followed Whacker to their left along the narrow gallery toward the stairs down to the studio, she could hear Walkie-Talkie close behind her. She grabbed at the hand rail above the open space on her right to speed her on her way and stumbled. For a second she had a glimpse of the lighting grid sliding away as she fell forward to sprawl diagonally across the gallery, her head stuck out beneath the rail.

She could see the top of the studio sets, far below her as she clutched the edge of the gallery for support, her stomach heaving. Then she felt Walkie-Talkie's hands seizing her legs. He was forcing her forward into space. She felt her grip begin to loosen and screamed.

Suddenly the pressure on her legs eased and she used the last of her strength to heave herself backwards to safety.

"What happened?" asked a man's voice from close by and she looked up to see Theo standing above her. Only then did she realize that she was outside the glass partition which separated the Production Control Room from the gallery.

"She tripped," she heard Walkie-Talkie explaining. "Luckily for her I was close enough to grab her or she would have gone over the edge of the gallery."

Maura got to her feet, still dazed at the thought that she might now have been lying on the studio floor with her neck broken.

"This isn't a children's playground," Theo snapped, "and she's no business here anyway. Will you please see that in future no-one gets into studio unless they're involved in the production?"

"Of course, boss. I'm sorry. I don't know how she got here in the first place."

"Well, it's your job to know. Suppose anything had happened to her? I doubt if she would even have been covered by insurance when she had no legitimate reason for being here."

"I came to meet Whacker," Maura mumbled. "We were going to go home together."

"Whacker?" Theo looked around and saw him, standing on the gallery stairs, where he had stopped dead at the sound of Maura's scream.

"I see," Theo said. "Well, my invitation was to him only. He had no right to bring anyone else in. In any case, the recording is long over now. Get along home, both of you, and don't ever set foot in a studio again unless you're scheduled in for a rehearsal or a recording."

"I'm sorry." Whacker's face reddened in dismay, but Maura had no wish to stay. As Theo turned away towards the Production

Control Room door, she thought only of getting off the gallery before Theo's absence might give Walkie-Talkie another opportunity to push her over. She hurried Whacker on down the stairs ahead of her, as fast as her shaky legs could manage.

"Let's get out of here!" she muttered as she urged him across the now deserted studio and through reception to the safety of the studio grounds.

Only as they reached their bicycles, padlocked to the uprights along the covered walkway at the side of the studio building, did Maura feel able to speak again.

"He tried to push me off the gallery!" she gasped in disbelief. "I might have been dead by now!"

"Danny Noonan was right," Whacker said. "He's worse than any old robber. And all over nothing more than a job!"

Thinking it over afterwards, Maura felt that there must be people like her father who would be almost ready to murder for a job, but her mind was still not working properly at the time.

"I don't care what it's about." she said. "I was never so scared of anybody!"

"Things are real bad," Whacker agreed.

"And Theo's not going to listen to anything we say now. He's black out with us and he still trusts Walkie-Talkie."

"How could he?" Maura shuddered. Her legs were still like jelly, so that she could hardly pedal her bike on to the Stillorgan Road. "You'd know just by the way he looks at you that he'd do anything!"

"The way he looks at *us*," Whacker corrected. "Not at Theo. He's all charm with him. I've been watching him all day, remember. And he *is* good at his job. He had everyone in great humour all day."

"Theo and Sylvia didn't look in great humour when I saw them," Maura retorted angrily.

"I know, it was awful. I got out of the Production Control Room fast, but they were having a desperate row."

"I think Theo must have hit Sylvia," Maura said.

"I don't know. I didn't see him do anything." Whacker pedalled in silence for a while, but then added, "But he was in an awful way. I'd never have believed he could get into a rage like that. He's always so quiet."

Maura thought again about her father. He never made jokes like Mr Kelly, or sang in

Flynn's so you could hear him passing down Ormond Quay the way you could hear Mr Doyle. If he had not got the price of a pint, he would sit all evening in front of the telly without a word to anyone. But he had hit her mother just the same when she had told him about Ma Sullivan.

"The quiet ones are the worst," she said, "because you're not expecting it."

"Then we've got to do something quick," Whacker told her, "before things get any worse."

"Worse? Didn't Walkie-Talkie try to kill me? I don't know what could be worse!"

Whacker looked at her for a moment.

"Next time he might suceed," he said. "Or he could keep on at Theo until he half-killed Sylvia. We've got to talk to Theo. We've got to make him understand what Walkie-Talkie's doing and why."

"Not me! I'm scared. Isn't it bad enough that I've to work in a show with a man that wants to kill me?"

"There's nothing he can do so long as you keep with the others and stay on the studio floor."

"Supposing he gets me in the dressing-room?"

"What can he do? He'd have to make it look like an accident, remember. Besides, they're not likely to give you a dressing-room on your own, with so many in the show. Just try not to be alone with him and you'll be fine."

It was all very well for Whacker, Maura thought. No-one had tried to push him to his death, but she knew she had had enough. From this out she would mind her own business and think of nothing only her part in the show.

She realized that that was easier said than done, though, when she saw the way Sylvia looked at rehearsal next day. All the bounce and bubble seemed to have gone out of her and she had a bruise on her left cheek bone that was only partly hidden by the thick make-up she was wearing. She seemed to be trying to avoid Michael, too, and only spoke to him when she needed to ask him something about a move or a camera position. He, on the other hand, seemed to be watching her all the time and this seemed to be upsetting Bea who was, as usual, watching him.

It was the last day in the rehearsal hall for this first programme. Next morning they would be in studio and Maura comforted herself with the thought that at least the

others would be with her then. She had
decided to ask the stage manager if she could
be in the same dressing-room as May and
Imelda. If she would not allow them to come in
with her because they were only extras, she
could surely go in with them, even if it meant
changing in the big chorus room with all the
dancers. In the meantime, she would soon
have Whacker with her.

They had got back to the Square the
previous evening to be met by Imelda to say
that there had been a message from Flynn's.
Michael had decided to put in the breakdancing immediately after lunch so it could be
included in the run-through, scheduled for
three o' clock. Whacker was to be at rehearsal
at two and Maura was looking forward to his
arrival. A spot of breakdancing might cheer
them all up, she thought.

It was only five to two when she got back
from lunch, but the door of the hall was ajar.
She could not hear singing or talk, but there
was a patter of feet as if someone was doing a
soft-shoe shuffle. The dancers always seemed
to arrive in a noisy bunch, like kids out of
school, though they were all much older than
Maura. It must be Whacker, she thought.

She pushed the door wide and walked in. As

she did so, the sound stopped abruptly.
Realizing it had come from the corner by the
piano, which was behind the door, she
turned—and heard the door slam shut behind
her. Then she froze in horror. Standing with
his back to the closed door was Walkie-Talkie.

6

A Long Shot

aura's mind raced as she looked frantically around her for some means of escape.

"Don't be alone with him," Whacker had warned and now here he was between her and the rehearsal room's only door. She tried to march past him, but he blocked her path.

"Let me by," she said, making an effort to sound confident. "I want to go out."

"But you've only just come in!" he mocked.

"I was looking for someone."

"So was I. And I've found what I was looking for. You and I have to talk."

The others would surely be arriving any minute, Maura thought. All she had to do was play for time.

"I have to get my script first," she lied. "I must have left it outside."

He laughed.

"Try your gaberdine pocket."

"What?"

Suddenly he grabbed her wrist, forcing her right hand against the script which bulged from her pocket.

"What's that then?"

"Let me go!" She tried to pull her hand free but Walkie-Talkie merely tightened his grip.

"In a minute. When I'm sure you've finally got the message. Didn't I warn you yesterday not to interfere?"

"Yes. And I've done nothing. Let go of my hand, please!"

He pulled her round to face him, his blue eyes blazing.

"What do you think this is? Some sort of nursery game? While you're playing hide and go seek someone could get hurt. Don't you realize you could have fallen to your death yesterday if I hadn't grabbed you?"

"You tried to push me!" She was indignant now.

"I wouldn't say that to anyone if I were you! Neurotic little girls with persecution mania don't get work on television! And that break-dancing pal of yours had better watch his step too. I haven't been a floor manager for ten years without knowing how to deal with messers!"

Maura struggled once more to free herself, but Walkie-Talkie's hand gripped her wrist as tightly as a wrench. Suddenly he twisted it behind her back, forcing it upwards so the pain shot up her arm to her shoulder.

"Ow!" Maura screamed. "You're hurting me!"

"Not nearly as much as I will if I have any more trouble from you!" he said, and though she could no longer see his face, there was an edge in his voice that warned Maura he meant what he said. "Now," he continued, "I'm warning you for the last time. Whatever you or your friend imagine you know, keep it to yourselves and keep out of my hair. Is that understood?"

"Yes," gasped Maura, bent almost double in her efforts to ease the pressure on her shoulder. "I won't say a word. I promise! Please let go!"

He gave her wrist a vicious twist so that she screamed again. Through the waves of pain she heard a babble of voices and footsteps on the other side of the door. Walkie-Talkie must have heard them too.

"Just make sure you remember, that's all!"

he said into her ear, as he simultaneously let go of her wrist and gave her a little push that sent her stumbling across the room from him, nursing her wrist.

By time the others arrived, they were far apart and Walkie-Talkie was gyrating like Michael Jackson.

"No wonder they call me Whacko Jacko!" he grinned at Roger. "Did you hear the way that young wan squealed? I should be in front of the cameras instead of wasting my talents as a Floor Manager!"

Everyone laughed and Maura knew only Whacker would believe her if she dared to tell them the real reason she had screamed. Walkie-Talkie hid his ruthlessness beneath the mask of a clown, she thought. Everyone loves a clown and he was obviously popular. Theo and Michael both trusted him and even Sylvia liked him. If she should be reckless enough to break the promise she had just made, not one of them would believe her story. They would all think she was mad—a neurotic little girl with persecution mania, like Walkie-Talkie had said.

Making people laugh was part of his job in a way, she thought. His joking helped to give confidence to the cast and to put an invited audience into good humour before a comedy or chat show. And he was good at his job. She had seen for herself how he had made everyone laugh before *The Late, Late Show* until panel and audience alike were in the mood to enjoy the evening. He had even made her smile, though she had been tense from terror. Little did she know then how soon he would become the greatest terror of all.

She shuddered, rubbing her aching shoulder. What did he mean to do next, this monster disguised as a clown, at this very moment surrounded by a group of laughing dancers as the hand that a minute ago had been twisting her wrist was flung upward to illustrate some funny story?

When Michael had arrived and seen him he had looked at his watch in surprise.

"The run-through isn't until three," he had said. "You're early, Jacko."

But Walkie-Talkie had even joked about that.

"Isn't that better than being the late Jacko?" he had laughed. "Time enough for that when I'm dead and buried."

He was never at a loss, never stuck for an answer. How could Maura ever hope to get the better of him?

She said as much to May and Imelda next morning in the chorus dressing-room, whispering nervously even though they were on their own.

"Are you just going to give up then and do nothing?" Imelda asked.

Maura flushed. Imelda was making her sound like a coward. As usual, May came to her defence.

"It's easy for us to talk," she told Imelda. "How would you like to have someone like that gunning for you? All the same," she added, turning to Maura, "it seems awful not to do anything to stop him."

"But what can I do?" Maura asked. "He made me promise!"

"Yeah!" May said, "but not me! I could talk to Theo!"

"It's too dangerous!" Maura shivered at the thought of it. "Anyway, why would he believe anything you said? You've never even spoken to him!"

"No, but Whacker has. We could go and see him together."

"Theo's off Whacker now," Maura said, "and anyway Walkie-Talkie will be keeping a watch on him. Probably on you too. He knows we're all friends."

At that moment there was a loud bang on the door and Walkie-Talkie himself shouted at them that they were wanted in Make-Up.

Maura went white.

"He could have heard us!" she gasped. "It's too dangerous to talk here."

"Then I know what I'll do," May said.

"What?"

"I'm not telling. You promised to stay out of it so you can just leave it to me now. Just think about the show."

The three boys were already in Make-Up when the girls went in. They were laughing and joking as one of the make-up girls showed Whacker how to spread the foundation evenly all over his face, while she darkened Richie's brows. They had no lines to remember. Apart from Whacker, who had already been given his positions and cues, they had nothing to remember at all. For them the whole thing was a bit of a lark with a few bob at the end of it.

Maura did not feel like laughing. She sat silently in the corner and tried to shut out the sound of the voices all around her, till the other make-up girl said: "Which of you is the singer?" and May pointed to her.

Then the girl came over to her and said:

"Weren't you in with us before?" and Maura
had to answer her and talk politely about *The
Late, Late Show* and her part in the series.

When she was finished in Make-Up, Maura
went into the studio. It was in chaos. In the
centre was part of the deck of the Holyhead
Boat, with its handrail and a lifeboat slung in
position. There was part of the quayside, too,
with ropes and bollards, as well as a section of
the boarding area and customs hall. In one
corner of the studio was a telephone box
against a wall and in another the interior of a
bar, with stools at the counter and tables and
chairs.

Stage-hands were busy tying lifebelts to the
handrail of the ship, while the stage manager
stood on the steps leading down to the
quayside with a check list in her hand.
Cameramen were swinging the heavy
cameras into place around the ship and one
flipped through his lenses. Another sat as if at
the wheel of a car, driving the big crane into
position. This had a camera mounted on the
front of it and one of the men who had come to
the rehearsal and who seemed to be in charge,
sat on a little seat behind the camera. As he
looked through his viewfinder, the crane
swung around so that he could swoop in over

the rail of the ship, hover like a helicopter and then pull away so as to look down at the stagehands from above.

Up on the gallery outside the Sound Control Room a man shouted down at the fat sound man who was manoeuvring the tall sound boom on its little wheeled platform. Everywhere people seemed to be doing last minute adjustments, touching up the paintwork here, bringing on props. there, while the lighting men were checking and angling the heavy lamps far above. In the midst of all the confusion stood Walkie-Talkie, laughing, joking and issuing instructions.

Maura saw Whacker, watching everything carefully as if he meant to remember the smallest detail, and she was going to join him when Michael appeared in the centre of the studio and clapped his hands for quiet.

"As soon as Jacko's ready we'll stagger through it," he said, when he could make himself heard. "This rehearsal is mainly for cameras, sound and lighting so you needn't waste too much energy. I'll be concentrating on exact positions and putting in the extras. There'll be endless stops and delays, but please be patient and bear with me. I'll be up in the box so if anyone has a problem talk to

Jacko about it. And don't wander off! This is a
big production with a lot of people involved
and I don't want to waste time waiting on
people so be ready for your cues. And even if
Jacko tells you you're not needed for twenty
minutes, don't go further afield than your
dressing-rooms. O.K.?"

Everyone nodded and Michael went off up
the stairs to the gallery.

There were chairs grouped around a
monitor in the corner near the door, so Maura
went over and sat down to wait. She looked
around for May but, if she were somewhere in
all that noisy bustle, which had started again
the minute Michael had stopped speaking, she
could not see her. What did she mean to do to
warn Theo, she wondered, but immediately
forced herself to think about the show instead.
She must not forget, when she went up the
gangplank on to the boat, to take that big step
to the left, the way Michael had shown her
yesterday, so she would be in the right
position for the camera that was shooting over
the top of the hatch.

*   *   *   *   *

If Maura had only known, May had slipped
back to their dressing-room. She had got

paper and a biro from one of the make-up girls and, in her round, schoolgirl hand, was carefully writing a note:

"Take care what you do before you make a mistake you may be sorry for all your life ," she had written. "Sylvia loves you and you can trust Michael. Someone is trying to make trouble for you and them."

May chewed on the end of the biro for a minute. She had a feeling she should not actually mention Walkie-Talkie by name. How was she going to explain? She knew she had no time to waste. It would never do to attract Walkie-Talkie's attention by being missing when she was needed in studio. After a minute's thought she added another sentence:

"Remember who was always around when things went wrong."

She read the whole thing through carefully and then, where she should have signed her name, she wrote: A FRIEND.

She had no envelope, so she had folded it the way she had folded the piece of paper that had come for Maura's father. She had called for Maura on the way to school just as the piece of paper had arrived. Maura's father had pitched it out of the door, refusing to write anything along the dotted lines.

"I'm filling in no forms," he had shouted. "Don't I have enough of signing my name down at the Labour?"

May had picked the form up out of the gutter and folded it carefully along the lines where it said "1st Fold " and "2nd Fold" till it had turned into a little envelope with a printed address on the front. Then she had posted it into the blue litter bin opposite the Corpo offices.

Now she folded her letter in the same way, tucking in the end, and where the printed address had been she wrote: "Mr Theo Sylvester." So far it had all been easy enough. The hard part would be delivering the letter. She would have to wait for an opportunity. If Theo had watched the recording of one of his quiz programmes, he would surely be watching the first of his new light entertainment shows. Somehow, she would have to get the letter to him during rehearsals.

It would be difficult to get up to the Production Control Room, to give it to him without being seen, but maybe he would come down on to the studio floor some time. She remembered how, in the Olympia, the

producer had come round all the dressing-
rooms before the first night to wish the cast
good-luck, and had even gone into the chorus
dressing-rooms where Richie and Mickser and
Imelda had changed. Of course, television
might be different. She hoped Theo might do
something of the sort. In the meantime, she
slipped the note into the pocket of her jeans.
Then she left the biro back to Make-Up.

* * * * *

About two hours later, she stood beside
Whacker on the set while Maura sang "Danny
Boy". Maura was leaning against the ship's
rails, motionless, staring straight ahead, her
eyes focussed on the image in her mind. So
strongly did she picture the scene that, as she
watched her, May too could almost see Howth
Head getting smaller and smaller in the
distance and wonder how long it would before
she saw it again.

When Maura had finished singing, they all
clapped, as they had been told to do, and then
Richie pulled a mouth organ from his pocket
and pretended to play it. One of the musicians
was really playing off camera and the rather
odd sounds Richie was making would never be
heard by anyone else, since the sound boom

had swung away from them after they had applauded and was now hanging just above the musician's head. This was the moment for Whacker to begin breakdancing but, just as he sprang forward, Walkie-Talkie cried: "Hold it!" and everyone froze as the musician trailed off in the middle of a bar.

Walkie-Talkie stood listening as a crackling sound came from his cans. Then he nodded his head and came over to May.

"Michael likes your reaction to the song and he wants to cut to your face in close up for a second or two while Maura's singing. Then, when he goes to the group shot he wants you to pull a tissue out of your pocket and dab at your eyes. Have you got a tissue?"

May shook her head.

Walkie-Talkie called over the girl from Make-Up who was standing by ready to put more powder on Maura's face if it got too shiny.

"Tissue, please!" he ordered. "Over here!"

When she handed him one he folded it deftly and passed it to May.

"Put that in your right pocket," he said, "and pull it out when I give you a hand signal." He listened again to the crackling sound and then said:

"Right! We'll take it again from the beginning of the last verse of Maura's song."

May pictured everyone at home watching her face filling the screen of the television set in the front parlour and then remembered she was supposed to be reacting to the song. She concentrated on Maura and feeling again that Dublin Bay was disappearing into the mist. When Walkie-Talkie pointed to her, she pulled the tissue from the pocket of her jeans. Then, to her horror, she saw a piece of paper flutter to the floor. It was her letter to Theo.

Quick as a flash, Walkie-Talkie had snatched it up before Camera Two, moving in to cover Whacker's breakdancing, could show the deck of the ship. The minute the red light went out on Camera Three, showing she was no longer in shot, and the sound boom had once again swung away to the musician with the mouth organ, she seized Whacker's arm.

"If Walkie-Talkie reads that we're destroyed," she gasped.

She was not even sure if Whacker had heard her, for his eyes barely flickered as he watched Walkie-Talkie for his cue. Then, with the letter still in his hand, Walkie-Talkie pointed to him and he sprang forward to the centre of the group. Suddenly May noticed Maura's face. Now, with the camera on Whacker, she was only a part of the watching group and May realized she must have seen the letter fall and Walkie-Talkie pick it up, seen May's horrified look as he grabbed Whacker's arm and somehow guessed what had happened. For a second she swayed and clutched at the ship's rail to steady herself.

It was no wonder she was scared, May thought. Walkie-Talkie was standing watching Whacker spinning, the letter still held loosely in his hand. For the moment he was too busy even to wonder what it might be but May knew that, the minute that section was in the can and they stopped to set up the next, he would look to see what it was. Once he read it, she thought, it would be the end.

By writing and dropping the letter she had played straight into his hands. There would be no chance to warn Theo now. Walkie-Talkie would make sure of that. And from the look on Maura's face she had no doubt he would carry out his threat to her. And May herself was in it now. Walkie-Talkie had seen the letter fall from her pocket when she pulled out the tissue and would know she too had to be silenced. They were indeed destroyed.

7

Zoom in on May

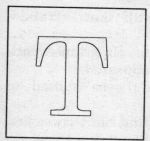

hen something happened so quickly that May wondered if she had imagined the whole thing. As Whacker sprang back off his hands for the last time, his left arm swung momentarily past Walkie-Talkie and, by the time he had ended up on his feet and Camera Two had panned off him and on to Mickser and Imelda, standing applauding beside Richie, the letter was no longer in Walkie-Talkie's hand.

So quickly had it happened that even Walkie-Talkie seemed confused. He stood for a second looking at his hand, as if he could not believe there was nothing in it. Then his cans crackled.

"Yes, Guv?"

There was a pause while he listened to Michael's voice and May waited, tense. Was

Michael saying he had seen Whacker grab the letter and they would have to do it all again? But Whacker had timed it brilliantly, just as the camera swung off him.

"Then you're happy with that?" Walkie-Talkie was asking.

May glanced at Whacker. He grinned back at her. The letter had disappeared.

"Right!" Walkie-Talkie's eyes shifted to them.

"Michael's happy with that but they're just spot checking the tape. Stay where you are until we get the all-clear. If the tape's O.K. we'll go on and stagger Section D."

Then he turned to Whacker.

"Did you snatch something out of my hand just now?"

Whacker gave him a look of surprised innocence.

"What?" he asked.

His cheeks were still flushed from his effort and his fair curly hair damp with sweat.

"I had a piece of paper in my hand. Did you take it?"

Whacker wiped his forehead with the back of his hand and looked puzzled.

"Sorry?" he said. "When was that?"

Walkie-Talkie's eyes were like gimlets but

he could not pierce Whacker's bland
bafflement. May wanted to laugh, but knew
that would give them away. She glanced
across at Maura and saw she was smiling. The
colour had come back into her face. Her first
song had gone well and Whacker had
somehow saved them from certain disaster.

Before he could say anything else Walkie-
Talkie's cans crackled again.

"The tape's O.K.," he reported and, as Richie
and Mickser gave a little cheer, he called to
the stage-hands to move out the hatch for
dance scene.

They were in that scene too, but even Maura
and Whacker were only looking on, like the
rest of them. After that, except for Maura,
they would all be finished. While Walkie-
Talkie was occupied on the floor, May
thought, she ought to be able to get the note to
Theo somehow.

As the stage-hands lifted out the hatch and
the cameras re-positioned, she edged close to
Whacker, who was again watching everything
that was going on as if he were already a
trainee floor manager.

"That was brill!" she breathed. Have you got
it safe?"

Whacker only grinned and patted the

pocket of his denim jacket.

"Can I have it back, then?"

"Too dangerous. Later. What the hell is it anyway?"

"A note to Theo. Warning him about your man."

"Are you bonkers altogether? Walkie-Talkie will eat you without salt!"

"I didn't put my name on it."

"You might as well have. Didn't he see you throwing it around the place? The safest thing now would be to get rid of it."

Before May could argue, Walkie-Talkie called them back.

"Michael wants you over here, chatting amongst yourselves. When the dance starts you can turn and watch." Then, into the microphone, he said: "Where exactly does this bit come?"

The cans crackled and Walkie-Talkie nodded.

"Yes. That's what I thought. Right after the breakdancing. Exactly. So he would still have his jacket off. Right."

Then he came across to Whacker, grinning.

"Take off your jacket," he ordered.

Whacker started to move towards the monitor. He could slip the letter from his pocket as he draped the jacket over one of the chair backs, but Walkie-Talkie was too quick for him. He had only taken a step when a hand shot out and gripped him by the sleeve.

"Hold your position!" Walkie-Talkie ordered. "I'll mind the jacket!"

For a second Whacker hesitated. Then he exchanged a quick glance with May. As he slid his arm from the right sleeve, he turned slightly on his heel so that the unbuttoned jacket swung back towards her. Under cover of his raised arm, May plunged her hand into the pocket. Her fingers felt paper and she quickly snatched it.

Pulling his other arm from its sleeve, Whacker handed over his jacket, but one look at Walkie-Talkie's face told May he had not been fooled.

"I said you were to hold your position, and that meant all of you," he snapped, grabbing May by the hand and turning her around to face Maura again.

"Relax," he said jokingly, though there was an undercurrent of menace in his voice. "You're all tensed up. Look at the way your hand is clenched!" He forced her fingers apart, but May's palm was empty.

Richie had had no idea what had been going

on, but he had seen his sister whispering to Whacker and knew Walkie-Talkie was up to no good. When he had suddenly felt a piece of folded paper thrust into his hand he had known better than to react. Without looking to see where it had come from, he closed his hand over it. They had played such games often enough. Before Walkie-Talkie could even shift his attention from May to Richie, the letter was in Mickser's pocket.

Walkie-Talkie's cans crackled again.

"Right, Michael. Right! he said and turned away, calling: "Can we have the dancers on the set, please!"

May grinned at Ritchie. Walkie-Talkie would be too busy now to search them all. The dance sequence took a long time to set up and even longer to record. If the dancers came out of their turns into the exact positions needed for the cameras, then the hand baggage they carried ended up in the wrong places. Even when they had all that right, something went wrong with the camera that was supposed to zoom in on Roger. By time they had the sequence in the can and the tape had been checked, it was the lunch break.

The canteen would be a good place to deliver the letter, May thought. There were so many

people milling around between the self-
service queues, the cash desk and the tables
that it should be easy to slip something on to
someone's tray or table then melt into the
crowd again so no-one knew where it had come
from. But though she kept a sharp eye out for
Theo while she waited for Richie to get them
both cokes from the cold cabinet and pay for
them at the check-out, there was no sign of
him.

Whacker managed to bag a table for six over
by the window and they hurried to join him,
unwrapping the sandwiches they had all
brought with them.

"Now," Ritchie said, when they were finally
organized, "will someone tell me what's going
on?"

"Ask your sister," Whacker said. "It was her
crazy plan."

"I only wrote a note to warn Theo what
Walkie-Talkie was at," May said.

"Only!" Whacker echoed. "Have you
forgotten that Walkie-Talkie tried to push
Maura off the gallery for less? If I were you,
Redser, I'd tear it up!"

"Oh yes, Richie. Do!" Maura pleaded. "Now
Walkie-Talkie knows there's something
written down that we don't want him to see

he'll just keep on until he gets his hands on it!"

"And I won't always be there to do a back flip at the right moment," Whacker said. "What did you do with it, Redser?"

"Mickser has it."

"Then give it to me," May said. "It's my letter!"

"You're welcome," Mickser said, putting his hand into his pocket. "And the next time you pass me something you might tell me it's hot before I'm in danger of being picked up for it."

"Hang on, Mickser!" Richie warned. "Your man's just coming through the check-out."

Maura looked round anxiously, but Walkie-Talkie joined a group of cameramen a few tables away. All the same, he drew up a chair and put it so he was facing them. Maura had no doubt he meant to keep them under observation.

"Go to the Gents," Whacker told Mickser. "You can tear the letter up and flush it down the loo."

"Better not," Richie advised. "Walkie-Talkie can do nothing while we're here. There are too many people around. But he's watching us all the time. If Mickser went to the toilet he could follow him in and get him on his own."

"Then let one of the girls do it." Whacker said. "He couldn't follow them, could he?"

"Slip it to me under the table," May said.

Mickser passed it to her and she wrapped it in the paper napkin on her lap. Then she drained the last drop of coke from her glass, wiped her mouth with the napkin that was folded round the letter, crumpled it a little and dropped it into the empty glass. Then she pushed back her chair.

"I'll see you outside," she said, standing and putting the glass on her plate with the knife and the empty sandwich wrappings. Then she carried them over to the rack where people stacked their used crockery. With her back towards Walkie-Talkie, she took the napkin from the glass and slipped it down the neck of her tee-shirt. Without turning round, she hurried on past the check-out to the Ladies.

As soon as the door was safely locked behind her, she took the letter from the napkin. It was rather crumpled now, but she smoothed it out carefully. She had no intention of tearing it up. Walkie-Talkie had already searched her and would be more likely to suspect the boys now. But even if he guessed what she had just done, he would think she was acting as Whacker had suggested. She would let the others think the same. It might be better if they thought she had got rid of the letter, but she would get it to Theo somehow. It was the only way. She would never have enough time alone with him to explain, even if he were willing to listen to her.

He had never come over to the canteen. Bea and Michael had arrived late, joining the table where Roger sat with the choreographer, but Theo was not with them. Neither was Sylvia. Maybe they had gone out for a meal, but there really had not been time.

They had only an hour and Sylvia was in the bit they were doing immediately after lunch. Wherever they had been they would have to be back soon. Michael, Bea and the designer were all together at a table near the door. Now, while they and the crew were all in the Canteen, she could slip up to the Production Control Room and see if Theo were there. But maybe Walkie-Talkie might follow her, if he saw her leaving on her own. Then she remembered that there was a second door out of the Canteen just opposite the door to the Ladies. It was round the corner from the telephone and out of sight of all but the corner tables. When you went out of that door you could not be seen through the glass wall of the

Canteen, because you came out on to the grass strip behind the wall which screened the Workshops from the Reception area. If she went that way and Walkie Talkie was watching, he would think she was still in the Ladies. She slipped the note back into the pocket of her jeans, pushed open the swing door and ran towards the studio block.

The studio was quiet, but not deserted. The stage-manager and the prop buyer were arguing about something just near the entrance, but they were so steamed up that they never even saw May as she edged passed them. She thought there was no-one else there and hurried directly towards the gallery stairs but then, out of the corner of her eye, she saw something move. It was the crane. It seemed to be moving all by itself, like the robots making the car in the Fiat commercial, she thought. Then she saw that the cameraman who drove it was there, manoevring it into a new position.

She slowed down, moving causally as if it were the most ordinary thing in the world for her to be there. She waited tensely for him to shout at her, but he too seemed preoccupied with what he was doing. Then she thought that he might not know that all her scenes were finished, or he might suppose she had permission to stay on to watch Maura. In any case, she thought, it was none of his business. He was not the floor manager.

Feeling more confident, she crept quietly up the gallery stairs, the note now ready in her hand. As she reached the gallery, she heard voices below her and, glancing quickly over the rail, saw that the crew was coming back. Quickly, she ducked out of sight and moved cautiously along the gallery until she could see through the glass into the Production Control Room.

Theo was there all right. At first, she thought he was on his own. Then she saw Sylvia. She was hunched over the desk, face downwards, her arms circling her head, as if she were sleeping. She had a lonely look about her, May thought, like a small child that has cried herself to sleep with one tear still on her cheek.

Theo seemed to be sitting at the desk, just staring into space. Then, May realized he was looking at one of the monitors. The picture on it did not seem to have anything to do with their show. Maybe it was the programme that everyone was seeing in their own homes at the moment or perhaps it was coming from another studio. Then, as she watched, the blank faces of the other monitors lit up, with shots of whatever happened to be in front of the cameras at the time, like other cameras or stagehands moving about.

This was her chance. While Theo was absorbed in watching the monitor she could creep in, slip the note on the desk near his elbow and slip out again. As luck would have it, the door from the gallery was slightly open, so she could even open it without making a sound.

She was half-way to the desk when suddenly the door from the passage swung open and she found herself face-to-face with Walkie Talkie. She saw his eyes widen and, without waiting for him to speak, she turned and fled back the way she had come.

As she raced down the gallery stairs, she could hear him burst out of the control room on to the gallery above. She took the last two steps in one great leap but, as she turned to run to the safety of the crowded set, her path was blocked by the crane. Now the senior cameraman was in his seat behind the camera, as it hung close to the ground. Behind her, May could hear Walkie-Talkie pounding down the stairs. She was trapped.

Suddenly she saw the little red light over the camera glow bright and she realized that meant that Theo would be watching that picture now. Out of her desperation an idea flashed into her mind. She ripped open the note and held it out in front of the camera.

Even as she did so, the camera started to swing gently upwards. It would move away before Theo had had time to read it, she thought in panic. Without stopping to think of the consequences, she clung on to the platform of the crane, trying to stop it from rising higher than the letter, which she was now holding above her head in an effort to keep it in front of the camera lens. But the crane was stronger then she was. Pain wrenched her arm. Instead of holding it down, the crane was dragging her up with it.

8

Cut

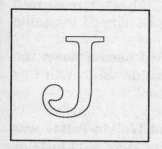

ust outside the revolving door of the canteen, the others had waited for May to rejoin them. While they waited, people they recognized from the sound and lighting crews began to head back towards the studio. Then Roger and the choreographer sauntered by, deep in talk. When even Michael hurried passed, with Bea still making notes on her clipboard, Mickser grew impatient.

"What's keeping her now?" he muttered. He saw no point in hanging around any longer. They had done their work and signed their on-the-spot contracts. They might as well be on their way.

"I have to get back," Maura said anxiously, as Phyl and Dickie passed with the rest of the dancers.

"Yeah, but we don't want May to have to walk back on her own while Walkie-Talkie's watching," Richie pointed out.

"And you've time yet," Whacker reassured Maura. "Nothing's going to happen in studio until he gets there."

"May must have flushed herself down the toilet with the letter," Imelda said. "Will I go and see what's keeping her?"

"Do," Richie said.

Even the group around Walkie-Talkie was breaking up now. It was not like May to delay without good reason. As Walkie-Talkie and the rest of the group passed them on the way to the studio, it suddenly struck him that his obstinate sister had been a bit too quick to agree to his plan. Then Imelda came running back.

"She's not there!" she told Richie. "How could we have missed her?"

"Because she never meant to meet us," Richie shouted. "She's going to deliver that letter. Come on, quick!"

As they hurried towards the Studio Block, Whacker grabbed Richie's arm.

"She might have gone straight to the Control Room," he panted. "By the main stairs."

"You go that way, then, and I'll try the studio," Richie ordered, and Whacker took the marble steps two at a time while the others ran down the passage towards the studio.

Inside, everyone seemed to be crowded down at the far end near the gallery stairs. Richie was heading in that direction when he suddenly saw the picture on the monitor near the entrance and stopped dead.

The others looked to see what he was staring at and then they too froze in horror. Framed on the screen was May's message to Theo.

* * * * *

May felt her feet lift off the ground. Still holding the letter above her head with one hand, in an effort to keep it in shot, she clung grimly to the platform with the other arm, though it felt as if it were being torn from her shoulder as the crane rose higher. She was going up with it, as it swung out over the quayside till she hung suspended in space above the heads of the cast and crew. If she fell now, she could break her back, she realized in horror. Not daring to look down, she gave up her effort to keep the letter in place and clung on with both arms.

She became conscious of shouting and
someone screamed. The noise seemed to be
coming from above, below and in front of her,
but she was tiring now. Her arms ached and
she knew she could not hold on much longer.
She closed her eyes, concentrating all her
strength on keeping her grip.

The crane was moving again, making it
even harder to cling on. Then her wrists were
seized in an iron grip. In her panic she was
sure that Walkie-Talkie had got her, but she
was too weak to struggle. She forced herself to
open her eyes and saw she was being held by
the senior cameraman. He was leaning down
from his perch behind the camera and
shouting at her. But she could not make sense
of his words. Then she felt something slide
under her feet and, as the cameraman relaxed
his grip, she collapsed in a heap on the ground.

*   *   *   *   *

As Whacker ran towards the Production
Control Room, he could see the blue light
shining over the door. He knew that meant
that they had begun rehearsal again, but he
opened the door just the same. To his surprise,
the room was empty.

Through the glass door he saw people out on

the gallery, all looking down into the studio. Then he heard a scream and raced for the gallery door. Looking down over the rail, he was just in time to see May fall to the ground as the cameraman released her from the arm of the crane.

"Jacko!" Theo yelled. "Is she all right?"

Whacker saw Walkie-Talkie bend over May and spoke before he could stop himself.

"No!" he gasped. "Not him! He'll kill her!"

Then he realized his mistake. At that moment, with the entire studio watching, May was in no danger. He saw Walkie-Talkie lift her gently to her feet and heard him shout back:

"She's O.K., boss. She doesn't deserve to be, but she is!"

Whacker knew then that he had really blown it. To Theo, who still trusted his floor manager, his words would sound way over the top. From shock at seeing May lying there and Walkie-Talkie, of all people, asked to help her, he had cried out before he had had time to think. Now Theo would decide that they were all bonkers and refuse to listen to anything they might say.

But there was something that Whacker did not know. Theo had just read May's letter. It was a peculiar letter, but he knew she had risked her life to make sure he read it. What he might have ignored as some silly practical joke or lies written out of spite if it had arrived in the form of an ordinary anonymous letter had at least to be taken seriously now, and Whacker's slip had just filled in the missing name.

"Then get on with the rehearsal!" he roared back. "We've wasted enough time already. And tell the girl who fell that I want to see her right away!"

It sounded like a summons to the headmaster's office, Whacker thought, but it was what May had wanted. Now, at least, she would have a chance to talk to Theo.

Walkie-Talkie was pushing May towards the gallery stairs, but Theo shouted again.

"Not that way! We don't want her falling off anything else. Is there anyone down there free to look after her?"

Whacker saw Richie then. He had pushed his way through the crowd to May.

"That's her brother," he told Theo.

"Good!" Theo said. Then he shouted down into the studio once more.

"Get her brother to take her to her dressing-room and stay with her!"

Then he turned back to Whacker.

"Are you in this next bit?"

Before Whacker could answer, Sylvia spoke. Whacker realized suddenly that it had been her scream that he had heard as he opened the Control Room door.

"No," she said quietly, "but I am!"

Theo put his arm round her shoulder just for a second.

"Then you'd better hurry up and get down there, hadn't you?" he said. His voice was gently teasing, but Whacker suddenly realized that something had changed. Maybe May would not find it so hard to explain to Theo after all.

Sylvia smiled and suddenly all her old bounce came back and she was once again the larger-than-life star that Whacker remembered. It was like the moment in the pantomime, he thought, when the old woman suddenly turned into Cinderella's fairy godmother.

"Just watch me fly!" she laughed, and bounced her way down the steep steps like a rubber ball.

Theo looked after her for a second as the others went back into the Control Room and took their seats.

"Right!" he said to Whacker. "You come with me!"

As they crossed the Control Room to the passage he rested his hand briefly on Michael's shoulder.

"I don't want anyone resting on their laurels," he said, "but what you got in the can this morning was great!"

"It looks as if I've a friend or two on the floor," Michael said, smiling for the first time in quite a while, for he too had read May's letter.

"That's always something to be grateful for," Theo agreed, "but remember it takes a good director to inspire that sort of loyalty in a cast."

* * * * *

May was sitting in the big dressing-room she had shared with Maura, Imelda and the female dancers, but the dancers were all in the bit they were rehearsing now, with the farewells on the quayside and Sylvia's number from *Many Young Men of Twenty*. May was glad they had the place to themselves, because she still felt a bit odd.

"I'm cold," she told Richie, shivering.

"That's shock," he said, putting his jacket

around her shoulders.

"You're supposed to get hot, weak tea," said Imelda, whose mother had worked as a wardsmaid in Jervis Street Hospital and so knew all about such things.

"It's no wonder you're suffering from shock," Mickser said. "You must have been out of your tree to hang on to that yoke."

"Didn't it get me a meeting with Theo, though?" May argued.

The shock had not lessened her obstinacy, Richie thought.

"You could have got yourself killed," he said. "And then Ma would have killed me for letting you!"

All the same, he thought, May had done all right. He was glad she was his sister and not that know-all Imelda, but all he said was:

"As soon as you've seen Theo we'll go to the Canteen and you can get tea."

There was no need, though, as it turned out for, when Theo arrived a few minutes later, he had brought a cup of tea with him.

"I sent your friend for this," he said, nodding towards Whacker, "while I phoned the studio doctor."

"Oh no, please, I don't need the doctor," May said, but Theo told her it was only a precaution.

"And there's no need to worry about the cost," he added. "It's covered under our insurance policy."

Then he made her drink the tea while it was still really hot.

"Now," he said, "if you're feeling O.K. I think you and I need to talk."

"We can wait outside," Richie said, but May stopped him from leaving.

"I'd rather they all stayed," she said, "if you don't mind. They're all in it just as much as me and it's only that I was the one thought of writing to you."

"I don't care so long as someone tells me what's going on," Theo said. "It sounds as if there's a lot I ought to know. Let's begin at the beginning. Your note said someone was trying to make trouble for me. I want to know who and why."

"You won't say anything to him if I tell you?" May asked uneasily.

"I don't know," Theo answered gravely. "It would be only fair to hear what he has to say about it. Are you afraid of what he'll say to you?"

"I'm afraid for Maura," May explained. "You see, we're finished here now but she's in the whole series. And she'll be on her own, without any of us around to mind her."

"Does she need so much minding?" Theo asked, smiling.

"Didn't he already try to push her off the gallery?" Whacker burst out. "You ought to remember. You were there."

"Oh yes, I know what you're talking about now. But I understood that she tripped and Jacko managed to grab her."

"That's only what he told you! He tried to kill her!"

"I can hardly believe that," Theo said. "It sounds a bit extreme. Maybe he was just trying to give her a bit of a scare. But even that seems unlikely. You want to be very sure of your facts, you know, before you accuse someone of attempted murder!"

"I *am* sure," Whacker said. "I heard her scream and turned and saw him trying to push her over."

"It might just have looked that way to you," Theo said. "Why on earth do you imagine he might want to kill her?"

"Because she'd found out what he was at," Whacker told him. "When she realized, she was raging and forgot to whisper. He heard her telling me about it."

"And what *was* he at?" Theo asked. "He's extremely good at his job. In fact he's next in line for a director's job. He works very hard and doesn't have much time for fooling around."

"He wants to be a director now," May cut in. "He wants to make you get rid of Michael so as he'd get his job. I know, because I heard him say so!"

"Really? And when was that?"

"At the party after the last *Late Late Show*, when Michael offered Maura this job. He said it to the fat man with the pole that has the microphone on the end of it."

"The boom," Whacker corrected automatically.

"Are you sure you didn't misunderstand him?"

"Oh no," Richie said. "I was there too. We'd been in the audience because Maura was on the show. He was complaining that Michael got the job and not him, and the fat man said there was nothing he could do about it. And then Walkie-Talkie said..."

"Who?" Theo asked.

"Jacko," Mickser explained. "We call him Walkie-Talkie because of his ear-phones."

"Cans," Whacker corrected once more.

"All right," Theo said. "Go on. What did he say to that?"

"He said there was more than one way of killing a cat," Richie told him, "And that you might end up being sorry you had chosen Michael instead of him. And then he saw us listening and he said that little pitchers had long ears."

Theo laughed.

"That part rings true anyway," he said. "But Jacko wouldn't be the first to feel sore about not getting a promotion. I don't see what he could do."

"He already did it!" May said. "And it worked too! You just ask Maura."

"I will, when she's not in the middle of a rehearsal," Theo retorted, "but meanwhile maybe you could tell me what you think she'll say."

"Well," Whacker said, "for starters he got Michael drunk and made sure you knew about it!"

"That's right," Richie confirmed. "Maura said she heard Walkie-Talkie tell Michael that Sylvia would be hurt if he didn't drink her health after your wedding, although Michael told him he was trying to stay on the dry."

"And then he made sure you knew about it

and you reminded Michael he was still on probation," Whacker said.

"There was a little bit more to it than that, if you knew the full story," Theo said.

"If you mean about the fight," May cut in, "Maura thought Walkie-Talkie set that up too. She says he kept needling Roger into insulting Michael and then, because he was drunk, Michael hit him. Then, the minute they started to fight, Walkie-Talkie ran off and phoned the guards!"

"It sounds a bit fanciful," Theo said. "Surely Maura wasn't in the pub at the time? She must be well under age."

"Yeah, but she said the dancers were all talking about it at rehearsal next day," Whacker said. "And he made sure you knew all about it, didn't he? I heard him myself when I was with you in the box watching the quiz show."

"As far as I can remember," Theo said, "he asked me not to be too hard on Michael. That was the act of a friend, not an enemy."

"An enemy disguised as a friend," Whacker corrected. "He told you Michael had a drink problem and you looked to me like that was news to you!"

Theo looked at him for a moment and said

nothing. May hoped that he was trying to think back over it all, remembering how it had always been Walkie-Talkie that had brought him the bad news, like she had said in her letter.

"And then," Whacker said, "there was Sylvia."

May gave him a warning look. Whacker never had known when it was wiser not to say things straight out.

"Sylvia?" Theo snapped. "What has all this got to do with Sylvia?"

May tried to catch Whacker's eye but it was no use.

"He wanted to put you off Michael by making you think that he and Sylvia..." but by then even Whacker had noticed the look on Theo's face.

"Don't mind Whacker," May said quickly. "Sylvia only cared about the show going right. She was afraid Michael would make a mess of it if he was worried about losing his job."

But Whacker could not leave it at that.

"That's right," he said. "And Michael was afraid of that too. The day I was at the quiz show he and Sylvia were talking about it in studio after the taping had finished and Walkie-Talkie heard them. That's when he opened the mike so you'd hear them too and take it up wrong."

"I think you've said more than enough."

Theo stood up as if to put an end to the conversation, but Whacker knew if he left it like that he would only have made matters worse.

"But you still don't get it," he insisted. "I mean, I was in the box too and I thought the same as you did, but that's only because Walkie-Talkie made sure we didn't hear the whole thing. Maura was in studio and she said Michael was only asking Sylvia to try to get you to see him so as he could ask you for another chance and tell you he was giving up the booze for good."

Theo's face was white with anger and, for a moment, May thought he might be going to hit Whacker. Then he turned abruptly on his heel and left the room.

9

Super Closing Captions

ou eejit!" Richie shouted at Whacker, after the dressing-room door had slammed shut behind Theo. "Wouldn't a blind man see he didn't like you saying things about his wife?"

"I know," Whacker said sullenly. He realised he had just thrown away his chance of a useful job contact when he finished school. "But he had to know. Otherwise he'd never really get it all straight."

"Couldn't you have left it to Sylvia to tell him all that?" Imelda said.

"Look at who's talking!" Whacker rounded on his sister. "I never noticed you were behind the door when opinions were being given out! And he mightn't have believed Sylvia. The point was that we were witnesses. I was with Theo and heard what he heard and Maura

was in studio and heard what Michael and
Sylvia said. If he doesn't believe me he can
ask her!"

"I mean to."

They all swung round, abashed, to see Theo
standing in the open doorway. He sounded
calmer now.

"Thank you for being so direct with me," he
said abruptly. "I don't want to talk about it
now. The doctor will be here soon and if he's
happy you should get this girl home as soon as
you can. D'you want a taxi?"

May shook her head.

"I'm O.K. now," she said.

"Well, if you change your mind, ask Bea for
a taxi voucher. I have to get back to the box.
I'll be in touch."

Then he was gone again.

*   *   *   *   *

Back in studio, a very scared Maura was
speaking her first line. In fact, she was so
scared that she stammered over it. It was not,
in the end, having to speak instead of sing
that made her voice shake. It was knowing
that the others had gone and left her alone to
face the rage of Walkie-Talkie.

She was still shaky from the shock of seeing

May's letter staring at her out of the monitor and then May herself, hanging from the platform of the crane. Even when May was safely back on the ground, she had been transfixed with terror at the sight of Walkie-Talkie bending over her. Against all reason she had felt that May had only survived falling to her death in order to die by his hand. Of course, there was nothing he could do with everyone watching. Whacker had told her that. For the same reason, she knew she could come to no harm herself now. Yet, although she kept reminding herself of that, she was still scared.

Suddenly, it was time for her line.

"Is th-th-this the queue for th-th-third class, Mister?" she stammered. To her horror, she saw Walkie-Talkie coming towards her, but he only said:

"Can we take that again please? A little louder this time."

He seemed to be thinking only of his work. Why was he so calm after what May had done?

*   *   *   *   *

In the dressing-room, Richie had just found the answer to that very question. The doctor had moved May's arms until he was sure nothing was broken.

"There's not much wrong with you that a good night's sleep won't cure," he had said. "If the pain keeps you awake, you can take two aspirin. And, in future, try to keep your feet on the ground!" Then he had left, still laughing at his little joke.

"Come on then. Let's go if we're going!" Mickser said, but there was something still bothering Richie. Suddenly he realized what it was.

"The letter!" he said abruptly. "What happened to the letter?"

May took the crumpled note from the neck of her tee-shirt. Even amidst all the excitement she had remembered to hide it. Richie took it from her and tore it into tiny pieces. Then he stuffed it into the opening in the lid of an empty coke can that one of the dancers had thrown into the wastepaper bin.

"Walkie-Talkie musn't have read it," he said. "He'd have been really mad if he had."

"He must have seen it," Imelda said. "We all did."

"Because we saw it on the monitor near the door as we came in," Richie explained. "But everyone else was over near the gallery stairs looking at May."

"There's one person on the floor who must have seen it," Whacker told him. "The cameraman on the front of the crane. They were taking his shot when she showed the letter to the camera."

"He's nice," May said. "Only for him I might have fallen, and he never gave out to me afterwards, though I ruined his shot. We don't have to worry about him telling."

"Except for one thing," Whacker interjected. "He hangs around with Walkie-Talkie. They've been together at every break!"

"I still don't think he'd tell on me," May said. "He was really kind," but Whacker was already heading for the studio door.

"He mightn't know it was telling," he shouted. "We must hurry!"

But when he burst into the studio it was empty.

When the scene on the quayside had ended, Walkie-Talkie called a ten-minute tea-break. Hurrying after the others towards the small Studio Block canteen, he had caught up with the senior cameraman.

"You looked like Superman just now," he grinned. "I thought you must have dived from some skyscraper window to catch that young eejit before she hit the ground!"

"What the hell did she think she was at?" the cameraman asked.

"Trying to dodge me!" Walkie-Talkie told him grimly. "I caught her up on the gallery, if you don't mind! I do think if they're going to bring a bunch of kids into studio they should bring in someone to mind them. I haven't eyes in the back of my head. Anyway, I caught her outside the control room and ran her. I'm still on the stairs when I see her clinging on to the platform of the crane. Did you run her down with that yoke or what?"

"She was showing some crazy letter to the camera, just as we were going up," the cameraman said.

Walkie-Talkie stiffened.

"What did it say?" he asked, in a voice that would have made anyone think he was only casually interested if they had not noticed the sharp turn of his head.

The cameraman shrugged his shoulders.

"Some kid's nonsense about Michael and Sylvia and someone trying to make trouble. I could make no sense of it."

To his surprise, he suddenly found he was talking to himself. The Floor Manager was disappearing round the corner of the passage ahead of him.

* * * * *

Maura was taken completely by surprise. Her little scene had gone well enough in the end and Walkie-Talkie had seemed surprisingly calm. He was still in studio when she had left it with Phyl and Dickie, and she had started to relax. Then, without warning, she had felt that vice-like grip on her shoulder once more.

She felt instant panic, then remembered she was with Phyl and Dickie. He could do nothing now.

"I want to talk to you," he had growled, as he pulled her to a standstill.

"Hang on a minute," she had said to the others but, to her dismay, they kept going.

"We'll get you a coke," Phyl had called back.

After all, they only had ten minutes and Walkie-Talkie was merely doing his job. There was nothing surprising about him needing to talk to any of them in private. They would think Michael had asked him to have a word in her ear.

The senior cameraman passed before Maura could think of calling to him and then the passage was deserted. She was alone with

Walkie-Talkie.

Before she could cry out, he clapped a hand over her mouth and pushed her through a swing door beside them. She had just time to feel a chill and see a dark stairway leading upwards ahead of her, when he flung her forward with such force that she ended up on her knees on the stone steps, their hard edges scraping her legs. She tried to struggle to her feet, but a heavy weight pressed her body down until she lay sprawled face downwards on the stairs with Walkie-Talkie's knee on her back.

"Now," he snarled, "what was in that letter?"

"I don't know," Maura lied. "I didn't write it."

"Of course you know. And if you want to finish this show you'd better tell me quick!"

He grabbed a handful of hair and yanked her head back sharply, twisting it sideways so she was forced to look into his blazing eyes.

"Or have I to demonstrate what will happen if you don't?"

"It was a warning to Theo," Maura sobbed.

"About me?"

"It never mentioned you! Please let me go!"

"When I've got the whole story out of you

and not a moment sooner. What *did* it say?"

"Only that someone was trying to make trouble and not to believe anything he heard against Michael and Sylvia."

"So Theo knew that when he said he wanted to talk to that mad friend of yours!" Walkie-Talkie had it straight now, and he barely hesitated. "Right, so you're going to go to Theo and tell him it's all lies!"

"I can't!" Maura sobbed.

"You can and you will!" he snapped. "You're the only who saw or heard anything. You may not have written the letter, but anything the others knew they got from you. So you're going to tell him you made the whole thing up."

"He'll know that's not true. Why would I do that?"

"Out of spite, because I gave out to you for being up on the gallery. And because you're a silly little schoolgirl playing silly games instead of really wanting to learn how to perform on television. And you'd better make it sound good so that he *does* believe you. Because if he doesn't you're going to trip on that gallery a second time and this time there will be no-one there to grab you!"

* * * * *

Whacker ran straight through the empty studio and out into the great cavernous space beyond, which served the same purpose as the scene dock did for the Olympia. There, pieces of scenery were stacked on trolleys ready to wheel into Studio Two next door, while lighting equipment and spare cameras stood in rows in the gloom of their separate metal cages.

This place, too, seemed deserted. Whacker was about to hurry out through the huge open folding doors at the side of the studio block into the yard near the workshops and the canteen where they had lunched, when a small figure emerged from behind what looked like a whole pub wall on wheels. It was the designer.

"Where's everyone from Studio One?" he gasped.

"On a tea break. Try the canteen."

He hurried on, but she stopped him in his tracks.

"The big canteen's closed now. They've gone to the small one. Along the passage past the dressing-rooms and turn left."

He turned and ran back into the studio, colliding with the others who had followed him.

"This way!" he panted and they all turned and ran back the way they had come.

They found the small, carpeted canteen, but there was no sign of Maura, either at the counter or in the groups around the tables. Whacker hurried over to Phyl.

"Where's Maura?" he asked, and realized he was shouting.

"She's on her way." Phyl sounded surprised at his urgency. "She only stopped to talk to Jacko."

She was even more surprised at the reaction.

"Try every door on both sides of the passage," Richie ordered. "I'll take this side," and the group split up, bursting open the dressing-room doors without waiting for permission and racing on without apologies when they found Maura was not there.

It was May who pushed open the heavy swing door which led to the back stairs. She saw only a man's back, bent over something huddled on the stone steps, but the earphones were unmistakable. She screamed.

Then everything happened very fast. Walkie-Talkie half-rose at the sound, just as Whacker hurled himself on to him like a human cannonball. They both fell sideways

against the stairwell struggling, as May ran
to help Maura to her feet.

Whacker was burly, but Walkie-Talkie
seemed to be made of steel wire. He twisted
Whacker around until he had him pinned up
against the wall.

"You interfering little brat," he raged,
"D'you think I'm going to let you stop me now?
I'll make you sorry you were ever born!"

Then Richie, Mickser and Imelda burst in
through the door and flung themselves on
him. Even Walkie-Talkie was no match for
four and he was starting to get the worst of it
when they all suddenly heard a voice from
high above them.

"Stop that at once!"

Standing on the angle of the steep stone
stairway above them was Theo. The
struggling heap fell apart into five surprised
and confused people. Walkie-Talkie, looking
embarrassed, picked up his cans, which had
fallen off in the struggle, and straightened his
jacket.

"Sorry, boss," he began, "but these bloody
kids…"

Theo did not allow him to finish.

"I'll talk to all of you later," he said. "In the
meantime, get back into studio at once. We've

a programme to finish. And any of you not needed anymore go home now!"

There was such a mixture of anger and authority in his voice that no-one even thought of arguing. And it was a rather depressed and bedraggled little group that returned to the Square.

"He was only furious!" May told old Danny Noonan, who was sitting outside his home in the evening sun, waiting to hear how they had got on.

"Yeah!" Whacker agreed. "We've really blown it now! I thought when he came back into the dressing-room that time, maybe he might find a job for me after all, but not now. He was raging!"

"Why wouldn't he be?" the old sailor asked. "First you tell him his Floor Manager's out to wreck his show and maybe his marriage too, because he wants the director sacked. Then, before he's had time to catch his breath, it looks like he's going to have to do the rest of the programme with his Floor Manager in plaster—that's if he can still so much as see the cameras, after Imelda there has finished clawing his eyes out!"

"But it wasn't our fault!" Imelda cried. "We were only saving Maura from Walkie-Talkie.

But Theo never gave us a chance to tell him that."

"Maybe he didn't need telling," Danny suggested. "He sounds like a man would know the difference between a dog and a bone."

"Then why was he so angry with us?" Richie asked.

"And who says it was you he was angry with?" The old man took a long pull on his pipe before continuing. "He wasn't going to start refereeing a fight with a programme to finish, was he, and a wise head keeps a shut mouth till he's sure who to bite!"

Whacker was not comforted. The more time he had spent around the studios, the more he had been sure that was where he wanted to be. He had helped his father often enough to know he was good with his hands and his father talked about getting him his cards, but Whacker knew he did not really want to be a plumber.

What he wanted now, more than anything in the world, was to be a floor manger but, failing that, to get any job at all in television. He was absolutely sure now that he would only be happy if he could work in that unreal world where artists and technicians spent their time together making the shadows that became the focus of attention in tens of thousands of homes.

Yet now he had a black mark against his name before he was even old enough to apply for an interview. When Imelda started to describe Gloria's dress and their mother wanted to know if they had seen Pat Kenny, he pushed his plate away and went in search of Richie.

As darkness fell, the two of them stood talking in the doorway of the Byrne's house, while Patchie growled angrily at a stick which he was letting on was a rat. Then they saw Maura, pedalling her bike betwen the two posts that kept cars from driving into the Square. She saw them and swerved her bike into the curbside.

"Did you get finished in time?" Richie asked.

Maura nodded. Her cheeks, usually so pale against the red-gold of her hair, were flushed with excitement.

"I did 'Over the Rainbow' in one take!" she said, "and Michael was really pleased with me."

"Great!" said Whacker, trying to sound enthusiastic.

"And Theo talked to me afterwards. He said

to tell you if you wanted to watch next week's recording you can. I'm to let him know."

"Yipee!" Whacker's shout echoed off the wall of the flats and Patchie barked excitedly.

"Walkie-Talkie's not going to like that," Richie said.

"I don't think he'll be there," Maura told him. "He's going to Cork on an O.B."

"That's an outside broadcast," Whacker explained, as Richie looked puzzled. "So he won't be on the rest of the series?"

"No," Maura said. "I think he may be leaving RTE at the end of the month, only Theo said not to say that to anyone else. He only told me so as I wouldn't be worrying about next week."

"Will there be any extra work going?" Richie asked then.

"I don't know," Maura told him. "I don't even know what I'll be singing. That will all be decided at the production meeting on Tuesday. But there's twelve more programmes to do yet."

"Remind Michael that we're free if he has anything," Richie ordered.

"I won't need to," Maura said. "He said I was to say you would all be getting invites to the party after the final programme."

"Yipee!" Whacker shouted again, and this time Richie joined in as well as Patchie.

"Is May around?" Maura asked then. "I've something for her."

"She went to bed," Richie said. "She's O.K., but tired, and her arms ache."

"Sylvia said to give her this," Maura said. From the basket of her bike she took a box of chocolates. "She bought it in the shop in the canteen. There's a note with it."

Richie looked at the envelope that was sellotaped to the top of the box. The flap was only folded in.

"May wouldn't mind," he said and opened it.

By the light from the street lamp he read it out aloud.

"To dearest May with grateful thanks from Theo and me."

Underneath Sylvia had signed her name with a great big flourish.

"Isn't that just like Sylvia?" Maura said.

"Maybe May's not gone asleep yet," Richie said. "I'll take them up to her and then we can all have one."

"They'll keep till the morning, Redser," Whacker said. His invitation to next week's recording was more important than all the chocolates in the supermarket.

"And I have to get back or Mammy will give out to me," Maura said. "See you in the morning."

She got back on her bike and rode it around the Square to the opposite corner. As she opened the door of her house she could hear her father's voice. She must be very late, she thought, if he was back from Flynn's already. Then she heard her mother's voice. She was giving out to her father about spending all his money from the labour.

She was back in the real world. But only until the day after tomorrow.